What the hell am I going to do about this?

The question hung in Athan's head like a dead weight. He had to do *something*. That was inescapable. He had a responsibility to do so.

His thoughts circled back, homing in with his customary focus on identifying solutions to problems he'd ruthlessly analysed. Removing the woman who had so distracted his brother-in-law seemed the obvious move to make right now.

But what if—and now Athan could feel an idea start to germinate in his mind—a rival emerged for her attentions? Lured her away from his brother-in-law?

Dispassionately he made himself study the photo in front of him. As before, he felt his senses stirred by her heart-stopping loveliness.

Resolution filled him. Oh, yes, he could do it.

For one long moment Athan went on staring down at the image on his desk. Then, decisively, he flicked the folder shut. His mind had just made itself up.

It was a very simple, very obvious solution. And as the mental image of her lovely features flickered in his mind's eye he knew it would be very enjoyable.

Julia James lives in England with her family. Harlequin Mills & Boon® were the first 'grown-up' books she read as a teenager, alongside Georgette Heyer and Daphne du Maurier, and she's been reading them ever since. Julia adores the English and Celtic countryside, in all its seasons, and is fascinated by all things historical, from castles to cottages. She also has a special love for the Mediterranean—'The most perfect landscape after England!'—and considers both ideal settings for romance stories. In between writing she enjoys walking, gardening, needlework, baking extremely gooey cakes and trying to stay fit!

Recent titles by the same author:

THE DARK SIDE OF DESIRE
FROM DIRT TO DIAMONDS
FORBIDDEN OR FOR BEDDING?

**Did you know these are also available as eBooks?
Visit www.millsandboon.co.uk**

PAINTED
THE OTHER WOMAN

BY
JULIA JAMES

MILLS
BOON

First published in Great Britain 2012
by Mills & Boon, an imprint of Harlequin (UK) Limited.
Harlequin (UK) Limited, Eton House, 18-24 Paradise Road,
Richmond, Surrey TW9 1SR

© Julia James 2012

ISBN: 978 0 263 22804 5

PAINTED
THE OTHER WOMAN

PROLOGUE

MARISA gave a soft gasp as the man opposite her opened the slim case he'd just taken out of his jacket pocket.

'For you,' the man said. There was a fond look in his eyes as he slid the case towards her. 'I want you to have it.'

Marisa gazed at him, open pleasure in her expression.

She ran a finger lightly over the stones, which sparkled in the light from the candle on the table. 'It's beautiful!' she breathed. Then a more troubled expression showed in her eyes. 'But are you sure…?'

The man gave a decisive nod of his head. 'Yes, quite sure.'

Marisa picked up the case, reluctantly shutting the lid, gazing across at the man who had given her such a wonderful token of what she meant to him. She dropped the jewellery case into her handbag—the beautiful, soft leather handbag with a designer logo that was yet another such token. Then she lifted her eyes to the man again. She had eyes only for him! Certainly not for the middle-aged man dining alone, a few tables away, engrossed in texting on his mobile phone, his face in shadow.

Now Ian was in her life Marisa had neither eyes nor thoughts for anyone else. From their first meeting to this precious moment he had transformed her life beyond all recognition, and the wonder of it still amazed her. She had had no idea—none at all—when she'd come to London those short months ago how totally her life would change. Oh, she'd had hopes, it was true, and ambitions and purpose—but that they had actually come about was still wonderful to her. And it was all embodied in the startlingly handsome man sitting opposite her, gazing at her with such devotion.

She bit her lip slightly. If only she didn't have to hide in the corners of Ian's life, be hidden away from a censorious world like a shameful secret. Yet that, she knew, was what she would be seen as. Someone who had to be hidden away, never acknowledged in public, to the world. That was why they could only meet like this, in places Ian did not usually frequent, where he was not known or recognised, where he could be sure he would not bump into someone who would question her dining with him—someone who knew both him and Eva.

Eva...

The name echoed in Marisa's head, haunting her like a ghost that could not be exorcised. Emotion darted in her eyes. Oh, she thought in anguish, if only Eva were not who she was. The emotion deepened, and she gazed helplessly across the table at the handsome, smiling face opposite. If only Eva were not the woman who was Ian's wife...

CHAPTER ONE

ATHAN Teodarkis's eyes moved over the photographs spread out on his desk. His sculpted mouth tightened to a tight line like a whip, and anger speared him.

So it had started! Just what he'd feared right from the beginning. From the moment his sister Eva had told him who she was in love with...

He felt the anger stab at him again, and with deliberate control made himself release the tension steeling his shoulders, his spine. He contoured his back against the leather moulding of the executive chair he was sitting in behind the mahogany desk in his office. Across the wide expanse of expensive carpet the vista of the City, over which the lavish London HQ of Teodarkis International had a panoramic view, went unattended.

His hard gaze went on studying the photos. Though taken by a camera phone, and from half a dozen metres' distance, their evidence was indisputable. They showed Ian Randall, his boyishly handsome face gazing devotedly, eagerly, at the woman opposite him.

With part of his mind Athan could see why.

She was blonde, like Ian, fair-skinned and heart-stoppingly lovely. Her pale hair fell like a waterfall either side of her face. Perfect features—full parted lips, delicate nose and luminous blue eyes—all made her a total peach of a female. No wonder she'd captivated the fool sitting opposite her.

It had been entirely predictable. Right from the start Athan had feared that Ian Randall was weak, self-indulgent, and born to be a philanderer.

Just like his father.

Martin Randall had been notorious—notorious for womanising, notorious for succumbing to every tempting female who passed in front of him. He had indulged his incontinent desire for her until the next one floated by. Then he'd dropped the present incumbent and gone after a new one.

Time and time again.

Disgust and contempt twisted Athan's mouth. If that was what Martin's son was going to be like, then—

Then I damn well should have stopped Eva marrying him! Whatever it took, I should have stopped it!

But he hadn't—he had given the son the benefit of the doubt, even though it had gone against all his instincts to do so. His mouth set. And now he'd been proved right all along. Ian was no better than his father.

Philanderer. Womaniser. Libertine.

Adulterer.

With an angry impulse Athan got to his feet, picking up the innocuous-looking buff folder that contained enough dynamite to blow apart Ian's marriage. Could it yet be saved?

Athan speculated. How far had his adultery progressed? Certainly his *inamorata* had been installed in a fancy apartment by Ian, and judging by her designer outfit and freshly styled hair—not to mention the diamond necklace she'd been presented with—she was clearly benefiting from his largesse already. His mouth thinned. But had she paid the bill for that largesse yet?

The expression on Ian's face caught by the camera phone was—no other word for it—besotted. It wasn't the expression of a lascivious lecher—it was the expression of a man caught in the toils of a woman he could not bring himself to resist. A woman he was showering his wealth upon. But not, as yet, very much of his time. That was the one cause for optimism Athan could see in this whole sordid business.

The surveillance reports had found no evidence that Ian Randall visited the girl in her fancy apartment—not yet, at any rate—and nor did he take her to hotels. So far the only time he spent with her was in restaurants, clearly chosen for their out-of-the-way locations, and his only visible adultery was his besotted expression.

Can I stop this in its tracks? Can I stop it in time?

That was the question in the forefront of Athan's brain. Ian Randall was, it seemed, playing it pretty cautiously—in that, at least, he was unlike his father, who had been totally blatant about *his* affairs. But if that look of slavish devotion on his face was anything to go by he would soon throw caution to the winds and make the girl his mistress in fact as well as intention.

It was inevitable.

He set the folder back on the desk with a sense of angry frustration.

What the hell am I going to do about this?

The question hung in his head like a dead weight. He had to do something—that was inescapable. He had a responsibility to do so. If he had done from the outset what he'd wanted to do—put his foot down and objected to Eva's marriage to Ian Randall—then he wouldn't be facing this infernal situation now. He should have gone with his instincts, stopped the marriage. Whatever it had taken to do so. Oh, Eva would have been heartbroken, he knew, but what was she going to be once she found out what Ian had done?

Athan's expression shadowed. He knew exactly what she was going to be—going to become—if her husband followed the same damnable path his father had so heedlessly and selfishly taken. She would end up just like Ian's unhappy, tormented mother.

Athan had grown up knowing all about just how unhappy Sheila Randall was in her marriage to Martin Randall, Ian's father. Sheila had been his mother's best friend since finishing school in Switzerland, and once Sheila's eyes had been painfully opened to her husband's ways she had poured out her unhappiness into his mother's ears.

'Poor Sheila' had become a permanent fixture in their lives during his youth, as his mother did her best to comfort and console her friend—whether by phone or on mutually exchanged visits between London and Athens. Athan's mother had spent, so it seemed to him, an interminable amount of time trying to mop up Sheila Randall's tears, but despite his own sense that the best course of action would have been to divorce Martin Randall and be done with him, Sheila, it seemed, was of a romantic disposition.

Despite all the evidence she'd gone on hoping that her husband would one day realise that his wife was the only woman who truly loved him and his adulterous lifestyle would be finally abandoned. In this unlikely hope she had been supported by Athan's mother, who had been equally romantically disposed—a disposition also shared by her daughter, Eva.

This was the crux of his concern for his sister. His expression darkened. His mother had discovered the full depths of Martin Randall's irredeemability in a manner that had very nearly proved disastrous to her own marriage—and to her friendship with Sheila. For Martin Randall had been unable to resist the temptation of stooping so low as to target the best friend of his wife with his pernicious attentions. His attempt at seduction during one of her visits to his wife had, Athan remembered, caused an unholy row in both families. His mother had had to do everything in her power to convince her husband that Martin Randall's assiduously insistent advances were neither invited nor welcome, and it had taken almost as much persuasion to convince Sheila Randall as well.

A hard, brooding emotion filled him. Men like Martin Randall caused misery and torment and trouble all round. He had very nearly succeeded in breaking up his parents' marriage. If his son were *anything* like him he would wreak the same kind of devastation all around him.

But there was no way—*no way*—he was going to let Ian do that kind of damage. No way Ian was going to repeat his father's misdeeds. Athan would stop him in his tracks.

Whatever it took.

An angry rasp escaped him. If only Eva weren't married to Martin Randall's son! If only she could see through him the way he could himself. But Ian Randall's dangerously easy charm had fooled Eva just as it had fooled his own mother—Sheila.

Ian Randall had grown up the apple of his mother's eye, indulged and petted—especially after his father's early death. And with his good looks and his supreme confidence in his own ability to attract females he'd cut a swathe through the population as a teenager and a young man.

Yet again Athan's expression darkened. Had he had the slightest idea of just how dangerously indulged and doted upon Ian Randall was by his mother, he would never have let Eva get anywhere near him. But when *his* mother had so tragically died, when his sister was only just eighteen, Sheila Randall's heartfelt invitation for Eva to go and live with her in London had seemed a godsend.

Having already lost her father to a heart attack only two years earlier, this second blow had been grievous indeed to Eva. Athan, who had had to take up the full running of his late father's business enterprise, had been worked off his feet, and his bachelor apartment in Athens was scarcely suitable for a teenage girl to make a home in. Nor could Eva be left alone in the family mansion, with none but the household staff to live with.

Moving to London, living with her beloved mother's best friend and changing her college to one of the London universities instead, had been a far, far better choice for Eva. In Sheila Eva had gained a surrogate mother who'd taken her under her wing, and in Eva, the now-widowed Sheila had gained a surrogate daughter to lavish her attention upon.

She had also, so it had proved, gained a daughter-in-law.

Eva had fallen head over heels in love with Sheila Randall's handsome, indulged son, and had set her sights on him.

Just why Ian Randall, with his predilection for playing the field, had responded to Eva's open ardour with a proposal of marriage Athan didn't know—but his suspicions were dark. Had Ian not been able to bed Eva without a marriage proposal? Had the prospect of marrying into the fabulously wealthy Teodarkis family been too overwhelming a lure for him?

Athan, however, was the only one to have such suspicions, he knew. Neither Eva, with romantic stars in her eyes, nor Sheila Randall, with her doting maternal devotion to her son, shared them. So in the face of his sister's ecstatic happiness Athan had, with deep reluctance, given the marriage his sanction, if not his blessing. He'd also provided Ian Randall with a plum post in the Teodarkis organisation. Partly to satisfy Eva, but mostly to ensure that whatever frailties lurked in Ian's make-up he, Athan, could keep a very, very close eye on his brother-in-law.

For two years, however, Ian seemed to have toed the line, giving every appearance of being a devoted husband. Now, it seemed, his true nature was coming to the fore. The evidence against his brother-in-law was damming. Ian was consorting, in secret, with a beautiful blonde whom he'd set up in a lavish luxury pad and upon whom he was bestowing diamonds.

His next move would inevitably be starting to visit her in her love-nest....the long-feared adultery would begin in earnest.

Restlessly, Athan twisted in his leather chair. He would not—*would not*—see his beloved sister reduced to the sobbing wreck that his mother's best friend had become during her marriage, hoping and hoping that the man she so unwisely loved would mend his ways. He would *not* see that happen! Somehow he had to stop Ian in his tracks. But how? That was the devil of it!

Oh, he could confront the wretched man with the evidence against him, but Ian would probably try and wriggle out of it—after all, no adultery had been committed as yet, and he would probably find some weasel way of explaining away the blonde's existence. And if Athan took the photos to Eva that would achieve the very thing he dreaded most—breaking her heart with proof of her husband's betrayal. He couldn't do that to her—not if he could help it.

That might have to happen but not yet. Surely not yet?

Besides, shouldn't he at least give Ian a chance—*one* chance!—not to go the way of his father? If he could manage to nip this incipient affair in the bud, find a way of deflecting Ian from it, maybe—just maybe—Ian Randall would prove himself a worthy husband for Eva.

I can give him a chance—and if he falls a second time then I shall be merciless.

The question was how to give him that chance and prevent him succumbing to what had every indication of turning into a full-blown adulterous affair with the delectable blonde he was lining up for himself?

The brooding look returned to Athan's stormy expression. This required strategy—cold, logical strategy.

A hard light darkened in his eyes. Icy logic sliced down through his synapses. OK, so Ian wanted to start an affair with this blonde—and the blonde, from the photographic evidence, looked every bit as keen as he did. Whatever was motivating her—Ian's obvious wealth and generosity, or his golden-boy looks and seductive charm—she was clearly very, very responsive to him. It would surely take little more effort on Ian's part to get her into bed.

Unless…

Thoughts moved across Athan's mind. Dark, ruthless thoughts.

When it came to adultery it took two to tango. The adulterer and a willing mistress.

His thoughts coiled and uncoiled like a serpent in his mind. But what if the willing mistress were no longer so willing? What if Ian Randall were not the only good-looking, wealthy admirer in her orbit? What if a rival arrived on the scene?

Cut Ian out…?

Slowly Athan felt his taut muscles finally relax, for the first time since he'd ripped open the envelope and the damning photos had spilt out in front of him.

His mind raced ahead, trying to assess whether what had crossed his mind could work. The answer came through loud and clear.

Yes! Because it simply replaces Ian with someone else. Someone else who can take his place. Someone else who is rich and has a track record of successfully wooing beautiful women…

For a moment he hesitated. Was this really something he could go ahead with? For all he knew the girl was genuinely in love with Ian Randall—she certainly had a sufficiently devoted expression on her face.

He pushed aside his doubt.

Well, if she is, then I will be doing her a kindness in removing him, in providing her with a rival to him. What possible long-term happiness could she find loving a married man?

He gave a tight smile. If his plan worked, then Eva would not be the only woman spared unnecessary pain.

His eyes went back to the photo in front of him. He let his eyes wash over it. She really was very, very lovely…

Could he do it? Could he *really* do it?

Could he really seduce a woman—have an affair with her—for no other reason than to achieve his aim of parting her from a married man's attentions? He had had many affairs in his time, but never for such a purpose! Was it not just too, too cold-blooded to consider?

His thoughts circled in his head, seeking justification for his actions.

I don't intend her to be hurt or devastated by such an affair. I don't intend her harm. I only intend to get her away from Ian, with whom she cannot have an affair.

The logic was clear—irrefutable—yet still his expression was troubled. Sitting here, at his desk, it was easy enough to set in progress plots and machinations to try and save his sister's marriage—at least for now. But what would he feel like when he actually had to put his strategy into action?

Once more his eyes washed over the perfect oval face, the celestial blue of her wide eyes, the perfect curve of her tender mouth…

As before, he felt his senses stirred by her heart-stopping loveliness.

Resolution filled him. Oh, yes, he could do it. He most definitely could do it…

For one long moment Athan went on staring down at the image on his desk. The beautiful, blonde face gazed ingenuously at the camera, all unknowing of its presence. Then another image formed in his mind. Female too, but dark brunette, with deep, doe-like eyes—eyes filled with love for her husband, whose attention was all taken by the blonde in the photo.

I will protect my sister whatever I have to do.

He had reached his decision. Now he simply had to do it. Neither flinching, nor hesitating, nor doubting.

Decisively, he flicked the folder shut. Opening a locked drawer in his desk, he slid the incriminating folder into its depths, making sure he locked it again. Then he picked up his phone. He needed to make a phone call to an interior designer. His London apartment was very comfortable, very luxurious, and its décor suited him perfectly. But right now he knew it was time to have it redecorated. And while that was being done—well, he would need a temporary place to live.

And he knew exactly where it was going to be...

Marisa headed home through the chilly gathering dusk of a winter's day, walking along the wide pavement briskly, but with a lightness to her step that echoed the lightness in her heart. Although busy with traffic heading both east and west, Holland Park Road was such an affluent part of London that she didn't mind. In comparison with where she'd lived when she'd first got here it was a different world. A cramped, poky bedsit, with a cracked sink in the corner and a grimy, shared bathroom down an uncarpeted corridor, had been all she could afford on her meagre wages. London was *so* expensive! She'd known it would be, but the reality of it had hit harder than she'd anticipated.

The money she'd set aside to make the journey from Devon and tide her over had all gone, but she'd blithely—and completely wrongly—assumed that getting some kind of decently paid job would not be hard. Certainly a lot easier than it had been in Devon, where even if she had commuted—lengthily—into Plymouth, jobs were scarce and hourly rates poor in comparison. But she'd discovered, to her dismay, that living expenses in London were punitive—especially accommodation. She'd never had to pay for accommodation before. The cottage she'd grown up in might be tiny, and dreadfully ramshackle, but at least there was nothing to pay there except council tax and utility bills. London rents, even for really grim accommodation in run-down areas were terrifyingly high. It meant that even after she had found a day job she'd still been forced to take a second job in the evenings to make ends meet.

All that had changed completely now, though. Her life couldn't have become more different. And it was all thanks to Ian!

Meeting him had been amazing. And the transformation he'd wrought in her life had been total. A glow filled her as she thought about him. The moment he'd realised what a dump she lived in, he'd waved his magic wand over her and the next thing she knew he'd organised for her to move into a flat in a de luxe building in Holland Park, paying her rent and all her expenses.

And the flat wasn't the only thing he was paying for.

The manicured fingers of her left hand stroked the soft dark tan leather of her handbag as she walked, and she glanced down at the beautiful matching boots she was wearing, feeling deliciously svelte in the *faux* fur-trimmed jacket keeping her warm against the chill February air. The weather here in the east of the country was certainly colder and crisper than it was in the west, but in Devon—especially on the edges of Dartmoor, where the cottage nestled into the side of the moorland—midwinter Atlantic gales could lift the tiles off roofs and rip the stunted trees off their rocky perches. Lashing rain could penetrate the rotting window frames and spatter down the chimney onto the wood fires that were the only source of heating in the cottage.

Wood fires might seem romantic to holidaymakers, but they'd never have to forage for kindling in all weathers, or lug basketloads of logs in through the rain from outdoor sheds, let alone clean out the ashes morning after morning.

Not that holidaymakers would ever want to step foot into a cottage like *hers*. It was no chi-chi romantic rural getaway, thoughtfully fitted out with all mod-cons for city folk used to comfortable living. The cob-walled cottage was the real thing—a farm-worker's dwelling that had never been modernised other than being supplied with mains electricity. It still had the original stone sink in the kitchen lean-to, and although her mother had painted the cupboards and papered the walls, done her best to make the cottage homely and cosy, Marisa had always considered it old-fashioned and shabby.

Her mother hadn't minded, though. She'd been grateful. Grateful to have a place of her own—even a run-down one. Marisa had always known how tight money had been as she grew up. Her mother had had no one to look after her…

Unlike her daughter.

Again Marisa felt a lightness, a glow inside her. Ian was looking after her—so, so lavishly! She was overwhelmed by it all. Overwhelmed by his insistence on providing such a wonderful apartment for her to live in. Overwhelmed by his giving her money to put in the bank for her to spend on herself, telling her to go and get her hair done, her nails done, any number of pampering beauty treatments, and to go shopping for clothes—lots and lots of clothes. Beautiful, gorgeous clothes, the likes of which she'd only ever seen in fashion magazines, that had been bliss to buy and which now filled the wardrobe in her new apartment.

And overwhelmed, above all, by his insistence that she must be in his life from now on—he would hear of nothing else, as he had said over dinner the week before, when he'd given her that wonderful necklace that had taken her breath away.

Her eyes darkened. For all Ian's care of her, she could only exist on the periphery of his life. Could never be taken fully into his life—never be acknowledged or recognised or accepted.

Her throat tightened. She must always remain what she was now to Ian. Nothing more than that.

A secret never to be told…

* * *

Athan glanced at the laptop set on the coffee table in front of him. His mind was only half on the report displayed on the screen. The other half was on the mobile phone lying beside the laptop. Any moment now it would ring, he knew. The security operative deployed to track his target's movements had already reported her progress towards the apartment block. The next call would be to inform his employer that she had gone inside the lobby was heading for the lift.

Logging off, he closed the laptop lid with a snap, sliding it into its leather monogrammed carrier case and picking it up as he got to his feet. His car, he knew, was already hovering at the kerb.

He would have to get the timing exactly right. He headed for the front door, holding his mobile, waiting for the ring tone. He paused by the unopened door. Two minutes later the phone rang. The terse, disembodied voice spoke briefly.

'The target has just entered the building and the lift doors are opening. Ascent to her floor will be complete in nineteen seconds.'

Athan gave his acknowledgement of the message and hung up, counting down the seconds. At zero, he opened his apartment door. Exactly as he did so, the lift doors at the far end of the landing slid open.

Ian Randall's intended mistress walked out.

Involuntarily, Athan felt his stomach clench. *Damn*—in the flesh she was even more lovely than she'd looked in the covert photos. Slender, graceful, luminous skin, beautiful eyes, hair like silk—a breathtaking vision.

No wonder Ian can't resist her!

No man could.

Even as the thought formed in his head he felt its corollary shaping itself—ineluctable, inescapable.

And I don't have to. In fact not resisting her is exactly what I am here to do....

He could feel masculine reaction creaming through him.

Up to now he'd had repeated slivers of doubt as to whether he should actually go through with the course he'd planned—his swift, ruthless method of cutting the Gordian knot of Ian's disastrous dalliance. Oh, his head might tell him it was the most effective, time-efficient and all round painless way of separating her from Ian, but what was the rest of his body telling him? Could he *really* go through with what he was planning?

But now, seeing her in the flesh, he felt relief flood through him. Yes, he could do this—there was no reason not to, and every reason to do so.

More than reason...

No—that was something he needed to block right now. He had a task in hand—essential, critical—and that was what he had to focus on. Most definitely *not* on what his own desires might be. His desires—whatever they were—must be the servant of his purpose. That was what he must not allow himself to forget.

He walked forward, his pace businesslike and decisive, simply heading towards the lift. She'd stopped right there, in front of the doors which were now closing behind her. She seemed momentarily transfixed, and Athan could swear he saw her eyes widen as she watched him walking towards her.

She was reacting to him...reacting just the way he'd hoped she would. Without vanity, he knew it was the reaction he'd expected. The reaction he usually got from women. It would be hypocritical of him not to acknowledge it—not to accept that what women saw was six foot of lean male, with sable hair, and features which, as an accident of genetics—nothing more, and certainly no credit to him—got a resounding female thumbs up. Oh, he didn't have the kind of blond, boyish looks that Ian Randall had, with his blue eyes and ready smile, but he knew that his own strong, darkly planed features had an impact on women that got him the kind of reaction he was getting now. Just as he wanted...

OK, time to stop assessing the situation and make his next move.

'Could you hold the lift for me?'

His voice carried the short distance to where she was still standing, apparently immobilised. As he spoke she seemed to come to, and automatically her hand lifted as she half turned to press the call button. Athan continued to close the distance to her, and as the lift doors obediently slid open again he dropped her a slanting smile of appreciation for her courtesy.

'Thanks,' he murmured, letting his eyes wash swiftly over her.

Not that there was much 'letting' about it. He'd have done it automatically, he knew. Any man would. This close, she was even more stunning. Her wide-set eyes were gazing at him, and her lips were parted as though she were slightly breathless. A light, heady scent of perfume wafted from her, just as enticing as she was...

He stepped through into the lift, pressing the ground floor button. A moment later the doors had closed, shutting her from his field of vision. He felt the lift descend, and just for an instant he experienced a sense of regret.

Regret that he was heading in the opposite direction from her.

Or was it regret for something quite different? The thought flickered through his mind, as he stepped out of the lift and strode across the lobby to his car waiting at the kerb.

Why does she have to be mixed up with Ian Randall...?

The question, just like the image of her standing there so tantalisingly lovely, hovered like an unwelcome intruder. Ruthlessly he banished it, bestowing on his driver, holding open the passenger door of the sleek black saloon car, a brief nod and sliding himself into the leather seat, setting his laptop case down beside him. Such thoughts were pointless and irrelevant. The girl had to be removed from Ian's orbit, and the threat she presented to his sister liquidated. As swiftly as possible. That was all.

His mouth tightening, he extracted his laptop and resumed his work. He was a busy man—a *very* busy man. The multinational company he'd inherited from his father, which was one of the major plutocratic mercantile dynasties in Greece, allowed precious little time for R&R. Especially in the current economic climate.

But for all that, he knew he would have to make adequate time to accomplish his mission to save his sister's marriage— at least for the moment.

For just a moment, no more, he felt that repeated flicker of doubt skitter across his mind. It was one thing to plan such a cold-blooded strategy when gazing at a photograph. Another to execute it.

Impatiently, he banished his doubts. It had to be done, and that was that. Marisa Milburne would come to no harm by his seduction of her. She would have an enjoyable interlude in her life, as luxurious as the one Ian Randall was offering her, and she would be none the worse at the end of it. He had nothing at all to reproach himself with.

Besides, playing around with men who were married was always a dangerous business. If she learnt nothing else from the experience she was about to have, that would be enough. She should never have let herself get as deep as she had with Ian—even if nothing had happened between them yet.

I'll be doing her a favour, getting her away from Ian—and in a way she can enjoy...

And now that he had seen her in the flesh, knew that she was as lovely as her photo had told him, he knew he would too...

Again burning onto his retinas came the image of the way she'd stood there by the elevator doors, a vision of fair-haired, feature-perfect beauty. For a moment longer he held the image in his mind's eye, savouring it. Then, as the words of the document he'd loaded came up on the screen, he sliced it from his mind and got to work again.

Marisa let herself into her flat, her mind a daze. It had taken only moments—sliding open the lift doors, stepping out—and there he'd been, instantly in her vision. Walking towards her.

Or rather towards the lift. A swift, purposeful stride that went totally with the image forming itself in her consciousness. Making its impact felt instantly.

Tall, dark and just jaw-droppingly handsome...

But not in the way that Ian was handsome. Ian was fair-haired, like her, with light blue eyes, like her, and his features were boyish, with a smiling, inviting charm to them that had drawn her in immediately.

This man striding towards her had been completely different. A head taller than Ian easily, and far more powerfully built. But lean, not broad, with long legs. And much darker skin. European, yes, but with a clear Mediterranean stamp that went with the sable hair.

And the eyes.

Oh, yes, the eyes...

Dark as obsidian—not brilliant blue like Ian's—and dark-browed. They had seemed, just for a moment, to be spearing her.

Then he had spoken—only a few words—she'd felt the timbre resonate through her. Accented—she hadn't been able to tell what accent—yet obviously fluent in English. Asking her to hold the lift for him. Nodding and saying a brief thanks to her as he passed by and stepped into the lift, the closing doors shutting him from her sight.

It had taken moments—only moments—for the whole incident to play out, but now, standing inside her flat, she felt it replay in slow motion inside her head.

She made her way into her bedroom, dropping her bag down on the bed, taking off her jacket and mechanically shaking it out and hanging it in the capacious closet. She still seemed to be in a daze.

Who is he?

The question formed in her head, wanting to be answered. There were only three apartments on her floor, and one was occupied by a sprightly elderly couple who seemed to use it only as a London *pied-à-terre*. She'd talked briefly to them once as they'd come in from a night out, nothing more than mild social chit-chat, and they'd given her, she'd been slightly amused to note, a swift once-over in assessment.

They'd seemed reassured by her, when she'd made polite noises and said something about having come back from the theatre. The woman had disclosed that they had as well, which had led to a brief exchange over what each had seen and some anodyne views thereon. They'd seemed obviously well-heeled, and had spoken in the kind of accent that people of their background did, mentioning that they were mostly based in Hampshire, but came up to London regularly for theatre visits.

The other flat on her floor was occupied by a Far Eastern gentleman whom she'd seen only once, and that had been over a fortnight ago. He'd bowed politely to her, she'd nodded her head in return, and that had been that. Since then she'd heard and seen nothing of him or anyone else.

But the man she'd just seen now had clearly emerged from that flat.

Visitor? Guest? New tenant? She had no idea.

And it doesn't matter anyway! she reprimanded herself, shaking out of her daze. *People around here aren't exactly gossiping over the fences. Everyone keeps themselves to themselves, and even if he is a new tenant that's probably the only time you're going to see him.*

Into her head, hard on the heels of the reprimand, came a lingering response.

What a pity.

Impatiently she sat down on the bed and tugged off her boots, exchanging them for a pair of pumps more suited to being indoors. Time to stop mooning over a tall, dark stranger she'd seen for all of ninety seconds—if that—and remind herself that she was here for Ian's sake, not anything else. Ian was the sole focus of her life and she had better remember that. She had so little time with him as it was, and every stolen moment together was precious. Speaking of which…

She checked the voicemail on the landline phone beside her bed. To her pleasure it was indicating a new message. She pressed 'play' eagerly, but as she listened to the message her face fell.

'Marisa, I'm so, so sorry! I can't make tonight. I'm really gutted. But a pile of work's come my way—some deal that has to be signed off by ten tomorrow morning—and that means I'm going to have to burn the midnight oil, checking through everything. If all goes smoothly maybe—*maybe*—I can make lunch. I'll text you late morning—'

Ian's voice cut out, and she stared disconsolately at the handset. She hadn't seen Ian for three days, and she'd been so hoping that tonight would be on. She'd filled the three days as she filled all her days now—'doing' London. But what had seemed an exciting prospect when she'd first moved into this fabulous apartment a month ago was, she knew, beginning to pall.

She felt bad that she should feel that way. Up till a month ago, in her pre-Ian existence, she'd worked non-stop just to earn enough to stay in London. All the sights and entertainments of the capital had been far beyond her. Now, with the magic wand that Ian had waved over her life, she had both time and a lavish amount of money to see and do everything that London had to offer. For a girl raised in the wilds of Devon it was a cornucopia of wonders. Things she'd only ever seen on TV or read about were suddenly available to her.

At first it had been bliss. Armed with a miraculously full

wallet—thanks to Ian's generous largesse—she'd been able to wander delightedly around top department stores and fashion shops, putting together a wardrobe the like of which had only previously ever been in her fantasies. Ian had been delighted, and warmly encouraging, and she'd read approval in his eyes whenever they were able to meet.

It wasn't only shopping that had beguiled her. London held so much more than shops, and she'd been able to do all the famous sights, take in the capital's great cultural and historical heritage, immerse herself in its wonders—from a breathtaking trip on the London Eye to a wide-eyed tour of Buckingham Palace and everything in between. In the evenings she'd sampled London's glittering theatre life, with tickets to musicals and plays, live performances with famous stars on stage, sitting not in the cheapest seats up in the gods but in plush, top-price seats in the stalls and dress circle, coming back to the flat afterwards not on crowded buses or tube trains but in comfortable taxis.

It had all been absolutely, totally wonderful!

But she had always been on her own…

Ian had never come with her. Never.

He'd felt bad, as had she. She knew that. He'd said so repeatedly.

'I just *wish* I could take you out and about, but I can't— I just can't.'

His voice always sounded strained when he said it, and Marisa knew how much he wished it were otherwise. But it was impossible for them to be seen out together. It was risky enough just meeting as they did, and she knew she could not ask for more.

I mustn't be greedy about him. I have to be glad for what I do have of him. He's been so wonderful to me—and I'm so incredibly glad that we met.

She reprimanded herself sternly as she got up off the bed and headed towards the kitchen. She must not be doleful and depressed when he had to cancel their rare times of getting together. And as for feeling sorry for herself because she was so alone—well, that was just totally inexcusable.

Look at where I live now—what my life is now. How easy, how luxurious. And it's all thanks to Ian!

Yet for all her adjuration to herself as she set the kettle to boil and popped the Danish pastry she'd bought into the microwave to warm, making herself appreciate for the millionth time how blissful it was to have a spanking new luxury kitchen to herself instead of the sparse, tatty kitchenette in her bedsit, or even the kitchen in the cottage, with its ancient stone sink and rickety wooden cupboards, she could feel bleakness edging around her insides.

Determined to shake it, she went through to the living room, made herself look around at the pale grey three-piece suite, the darker grey deep pile woollen carpet, the rich silvery drapes framing the window that looked out over the roadway. She gazed down over the scene two storeys below. The road was quiet, lined with trees that would bear blossom in the spring but which now were bare.

Cars—expensive ones, for this was, as her luxury apartment testified, an expensive part of London, where only the rich and highly affluent could afford to live—lined the kerbs. She was grateful that Ian had chosen a flat in such a quiet location, and so near to Holland Park itself, for despite the charms of London she was used to the quietness of deep countryside. The winter's dusk was deepening, and few people were out and about. There was a chilly bleakness in the vista that seemed to reach tendrils around her.

She knew no one in London. Only Ian. The other women she'd worked with briefly had all been from abroad, and she had been an obvious outsider though they'd been perfectly pleasant to her. She'd known London was going to be a big, busy place, and that she would know no one to begin with, but she hadn't realised just how big and busy a place it was. How incredibly alone one could feel in a crowd.

How lonely she still felt, despite the luxury in which she lived.

Angry at her own self-pity, she turned away sharply, drawing the curtains and lighting one of the elegant table lamps. A cup of tea, something to watch on the huge television set in the corner, and later on she would make herself something to eat and have an early night. She had nothing to complain about—nothing to feel sorry for herself about.

And I'm used to being lonely...

Living alone with her mother on the edge of Dartmoor, she had become used to her own company. This last year in Devon, having withdrawn into grief at the loss of her mother, days had passed without her seeing another living soul. It had taken well over a year to come to terms with her mother's death, even though the end had come almost as a release. Since being knocked down by a car some four years earlier her mother had been confined to a wheelchair, and it had been torment for her. But the accident had weakened her heart, too, and the heart attack that had taken her eighteen months ago had at least ended that torment.

And though the devastation of her mother's loss had been total, Marisa knew that it had given her a chance to leave home that her mother's disability and emotional dependence on her daughter had not allowed her.

But it had not just been her practical and emotional one needs that had made her mother so fearful about her leaving home. Marisa was all too conscious of the cause of that deeper fear, and before she'd finally set off for the city she'd gone to pay a last anguished visit to her mother's grave in the parish churchyard.

'I'm going to London, Mum. I know you don't want me to—know you will worry about me. But I promise you I won't end up the way you did, with a broken heart and your hopes in ruins. I *promise* you.'

Then she'd packed her bag, bought her train ticket, and set off. Having no idea what would befall her.

Having no idea that Ian would walk into her life.

Would change it utterly.

The microwave was beeping in the kitchen, signalling that the Danish pastry was warm. Roused from her drear thoughts, she walked into the kitchen to make her tea. She would *not* feel sorry for herself. She would remember how short a time ago her life had been so completely different from what it was now. She would have a quiet, comfortable evening in and be totally self-indulgent.

Clicking the thermostat a degree higher, she revelled in the central heating that kept the flat beautifully warm. Two minutes later she was curled up on the sofa, biting into the soft, fragrant pastry and watching TV. It was a nature programme, set somewhere hot and on the beach, and Marisa gazed at the shallow azure waters as the presenter informed her about its marine life. But it wasn't the marine life that made her gaze—it was the vista of the beach, a tropical idyll framed by palm trees.

Imagine being somewhere like that...

If only Ian...

She cut short her imagining. Ian could not take her somewhere like that. Could not take a single day's holiday with her anywhere, period. That was the blunt reality of it. He could rent this flat for her, give her that wonderful diamond necklace, give her the wherewithal to dress beautifully, but what he could not give her was time.

She reached for her cup of tea, making herself focus on the programme. The presenter wasn't British. He had some kind of accent. Lilting and attractive. She found herself trying to identify it. French? Spanish? She wasn't sure. She frowned. Was it the same kind of accent that man who'd asked her to hold the lift had? She shut her eyes to hear it again in her head. The presenter's accent was stronger, but maybe it was the same type. His appearance in so far as hair colour and skin tone was similar too. Reaching for the remote, she clicked on info for the programme. The presenter's name was Greek.

Was that what the man in the corridor was? she found herself pondering. It could be—it fitted his air of foreignness. And the flat he'd come out of had previously been let to a non-Brit. Maybe it was some kind of international corporate let, with one businessman after another passing through.

I wonder who he is? He's just so jaw-droppingly good-looking.

With a rasp of irritation she pushed the question out of her head. What did it matter who he was, why he was there, or what nationality he was? She'd seen him for less than two minutes, if that, and he'd done nothing but nod and say a passing 'thanks' at her before disappearing. She'd stared at him gormlessly for the duration, unable to control her reaction to his startling dark good looks. Given the way everyone kept to themselves in the apartment block, she would probably never set eyes on him again.

And if she did it would be utterly irrelevant to her anyway.

Clicking on the remote again, she changed channels and finished off the pastry. The evening stretched ahead of her...

Two hours later there was less of it left to stretch, but she was still feeling bored and restless. She couldn't decide what to do next—go to bed or watch a movie on TV. It was one she was only marginally interested in, and it did not particularly appeal. On the other hand neither did going to bed at nine o'clock, either. All around her the hushed silence of the flat enveloped her, as if she were the only person for miles.

She reached for the remote. It was stupid, wasting time watching something she didn't want to. She would head for bed and read something useful—like the newly published hardback history of London she'd splashed out on last week.

Buying new hardbacks was such a previously unknown luxury she should make the most of it. Besides, since leaving college she'd hardly used her brain at all—which was a waste.

And you really don't want to come across as some kind of country bumpkin to Ian, either. Even if he's not a raging intellectual, he obviously knows business, and current affairs and so on.

She clicked off the TV and gathered herself to get to her feet. But even as she did so, she froze. A sound she had never heard had penetrated from the hallway. The doorbell.

Who on earth...? Puzzled and apprehensive, she made her way to the little entrance hall. The door was on a security chain, and there was a spyhole too. She peered through it, but could only take in a distorted impression of a dark suit. Nothing else. Well, it didn't look like a burglar paying a call, at any rate.

Cautiously, she open the door on the chain, which restricted it to a couple of inches, bracing herself ready to flatten herself against it if someone put an intruding foot through.

Instead a voice spoke. A deep, accented voice that had the timbre of familiarity.

'I'm extremely sorry to disturb you...'

Without volition, she felt her insides give a little flutter.

'Just a moment.' She slid the security chain off and opened the door wider.

It was the man who'd asked her to hold the lift for him earlier.

'I do apologise,' he said, 'but I wonder if I might ask you a favour.'

There was a faint smile on his face, a slightly quizzical look. Marisa found it did strange things to her. Things that made her lips part and her eyes rest as if helplessly on his face. She tried to gather her composure.

'Of...of course,' she answered, trying to sound polite but cool.

The faint smile deepened. So did the sensation of fluttering inside her. Her hand tightened on the doorframe.

'I've just moved into the apartment next to you, and I've only just realised that I've made no arrangements for any groceries to be delivered. This may sound the most stupid request you've heard, but if you could possibly let me have some milk and a couple of teaspoons of instant coffee I would be in your debt.'

Dark eyes—ludicrously long-lashed, she realised as her brain spun idiotically in her head—rested on her, their quizzical expression at odds with the formidable air of command about him. Whoever he was, he was most definitely not one of life's minions.

He's the guy that gives the orders...others do his bidding. Snap to his command...

And respond to his faintly smiling requests as if he's turned a key in their backs.

Especially if they were female...

The fluttering inside her, the tightness of her hand on the doorframe, intensified.

She swallowed, managed to speak. 'Yes—yes, of course. No problem.' Her voice sounded husky, as if her throat had constricted.

The faint smile deepened, indenting lines around his mouth. Marisa's throat constricted again. Oh, good grief, when they'd been handing it out this guy got a double helping.

'It's really very good of you,' the deep, accented voice responded, its timbre doing things to her she could not prevent. Didn't have the slightest interest in preventing...

Jerkily, she pulled the door wider and turned away. 'I'll just—um—go and fetch them,' she managed to say.

She headed for the kitchen. Her feet felt clumsy, and she was sure she bumped into the corner of the sofa as she made her way through the living room to the kitchen beyond. She felt like an idiot, bumping into her own furniture. In the kitchen she fumbled with the fridge door, yanking it open and grabbing a pint of milk. It was semi-skimmed. She hoped he'd be OK with that. She hoped he'd be OK with her brand of instant coffee, as well. Not that he looked like an instant coffee type of man. Her eyes went to the terrifyingly complicated coffee machine that stood completely unused by the microwave. She'd bought coffee beans, hoping to try it out, but one glance at the instruction booklet had quashed her ambition instantly.

Oh, stop dithering, girl—just give him the milk and the coffee jar.

She hurried out of the kitchen, carefully avoiding bumping into the furniture. He'd stepped inside the hall, though the front door was still ajar.

'Here you are,' she said breathlessly, holding out the requested items.

'It's very good of you,' he said.

That faint smile was still doing its work. His height was making the small hallway even smaller. So was his dark suit and black cashmere overcoat. His presence seemed overpowering suddenly.

A thought struck her. 'I've got coffee beans, if you prefer. The packet's unopened. I can't operate my machine.'

Oh, hell, she was burbling inanely. What did he care whether she could operate the machine or not. Yet it seemed he did—a dark eyebrow had quirked.

'Would you like me to show you how? They can be fiendishly difficult.'

Immediately she stiffened. 'Oh, no, thank you. That's fine. I wouldn't dream of troubling you.'

His lashes dipped over his eyes. 'It would be no trouble, I promise you.'

His voice had changed. She didn't know how, but it had. And suddenly, with a piercing light, she knew why it had...

Knew it from the sudden glint in his eyes—his dark, deep eyes...

She took a breath—a steadying one that she needed. Needed in order to remind herself that a complete stranger—however much of an impact he was making on her—was standing inside her flat and signalling that he liked what he was seeing. Her brain seemed to split in two. One half—the half that was reducing her to a wittering idiot—reeled with the realisation. The other half was shouting a loud, strident warning to her. Time to pay heed to it.

She shook her head. A small but decisive gesture.

'Thank you, but no.' She held the milk and the coffee jar closer to him. Her smile was polite, but nothing more, her voice composed.

For just a second longer he kept that half-shut gaze on her, then abruptly reached out to relieve her of the proffered items, managing to take them both in a single hand. The other was holding a laptop case.

'Once again, thank you,' he said.

His voice had lost whatever it had so briefly held. So had his expression. He turned away, going back out into the corridor, pausing only to half turn his head towards her, standing ready to close the door.

'Goodnight,' he said.

She kept her face composed. 'Goodnight,' she answered back. Then closed the door.

Outside, Athan stood a moment, his eyes faintly narrowed. *Interesting,* he thought. She had responded to him—no doubt about that. Years of experience had taught him exactly when a woman found him attractive. But she had quite definitely drawn the line when he'd made his second gambit, offering to show her how to use the coffee machine.

And if she hadn't? If she'd let me into her flat, let me make fresh coffee—shared it with me. Let me move on to my

*third gambit—suggesting I order dinner to be delivered so
we could dine together?*

If she had, what would he have done?

Would I have stayed the night with her if she'd let me?

For one vivid instant, an image filled his head.

Pale golden hair spread loose across a white pillow. A
slender, naked body offered to him. A lovely face alight with
pleasure…pleasure that he could give her.

Abruptly, he started to walk to his apartment door, jug-
gling with the damn milk and coffee that threatened to tumble
to the ground in order to extract his keys. As he stepped inside he felt another stab of hunger. But this time for the more
mundane fare of food. Well, he'd make coffee—even if only
instant—and consult the internet to get some food delivered.
There must be a catering company around that would oblige.

It was a nuisance, he mused, that the apartment block had
no concierge who could take care of that sort of thing for
him. But on the other hand a concierge was the last thing he
needed—they were the kind of individuals who swiftly discovered too much about their tenants. And if there was one
overriding necessity right now it was that his beautiful blonde
fellow tenant should not have any source of information about
him that he did not care to impart to her.

Least of all that he knew about her relationship with Ian
Randall.

And why he was going to end it.

Marisa didn't sleep well. She tossed and turned restlessly.
She might wish it was because she was disappointed not to
have met up with Ian last night but she knew it wasn't because of that.

It was because of that man—that tall, dark, ludicrously
handsome man—who had appeared at her door that evening.

*With the corniest chat-up line in the book! That's what
I've got to remember!*

Good grief, couldn't he have come up with something more original than borrowing a pint of milk? And coffee, she reminded herself waspishly. The problem was, try as she might to be derisive about it and label it nothing more than a transparent ploy, another thought kept intruding.

That any man with those devastating looks wouldn't even have to crook his little finger to have every female for miles around come running.

Pick up lines, let alone corny ones, wouldn't even be in his ball park. He'd never be reduced to resorting to something so clichéd. Besides, she reasoned, he'd seen her come out of the lift and might well have assumed she had a flat on this floor, but for all he'd have known she might have had the flat the elderly couple occupied. As a new tenant he wouldn't know, would he? Which meant that his ring on her doorbell and his request had been genuine, and not a pick-up routine.

Anyway, what did it matter?

But he did do that bit offering to show me how the coffee machine worked.

No, that didn't prove anything except that he was a man and men thought it inexplicable that women found machinery complicated. He'd probably thought he was being polite in offering—that the reason she'd mentioned she couldn't get it to work was a ploy in order to get him to offer help.

Oh, help, maybe he thought I *was trying to pick* him *up! Trying to inveigle him to come in...*

She squirmed with embarrassment at the thought. Still, at least she'd immediately said no, which was something to be grateful for. He couldn't possibly think she was giving him the come on, could he?

You behaved like a gormless idiot, though, don't forget— stammering and staring bug-eyed at him.

Yes, well, he was doubtless used to that kind of reaction from women. A man with looks like his would be.

And it wasn't just his looks, was it? Nor that to-die-for

foreign accent of his. If she were brutally honest—and she had better be at this time of night—it was the whole package that made such an impact. The looks, the cashmere overcoat, the bespoke suit, the whole Mr Rich thing definitely contributed.

And more than that there had been a kind of *aura* around him. That was the only word she could come up with. A kind of self-assurance, an air of being someone who gave orders, moved in the corridors of power, made things happen that he wanted to happen.

It was curious, she found herself musing. Ian was wealthy, and he sported the trappings of wealth from flash pad to gold watch. But he didn't possess that aura of power, that sense of being someone not to mess with.

A little shiver went down her spine. Disturbing. Disquieting. For a moment longer she gazed into the darkness of her bedroom. She shouldn't think about the incident tonight. Should put it out of her mind.

Should go to sleep.

But her dreams, when they came, were filled with the same disquiet.

And a strange, disturbing sense of anticipation...

Athan left for his office early. He always did, finding the first couple of hours of the morning the most productive before his heavy schedule of meetings started. This morning, however, he found his usual high level of productivity diminished. It annoyed him. Annoyed him to realise that he was finding himself replaying the little scene he'd created last night. Letting his memory toy with recalled images—images of the way her long hair had framed her face, tumbling down over her shoulders, the way she'd gazed at him, wide-eyed, the way her voice had been breathy and husky. The way she'd walked away from him towards the kitchen on long, slender legs, the fall of her hair waving down her back.

She really was very, very lovely.

Yes, well, he knew that—had already acknowledged that—and other than her beauty making it easier for him to carry out his plan there wasn't any point in dwelling on it. He had a mountain of work to get through, and it wasn't going to go away of its accord.

He also had to decide on a pretext for getting Ian Randall out of the country. The upcoming West Coast contract would fit the bill well. He could say it required input from the UK. He could even—his eyes narrowed in speculation—mention the trip to Eva. Suggest it would be an ideal opportunity to go with Ian, and then to take a holiday afterwards—fly on to Hawaii, for instance. Eva would snap at it, he was sure.

That would ensure he kept Ian well away from London for a couple of weeks, if not longer.

That's all the time I need with Marisa Milburne.

He had no doubts about his ability to achieve his goal. It was experience, not vanity, that told him women didn't say no to him, and there was no reason to suppose this one would be different.

Especially after last night. Any speculation that her attachment to Ian was based on love had been set aside. No woman devotedly in love with another man would have reacted the way she had to him when he'd paid her attention. No woman would have started the way she had, gazed at him the way she had, displaying that telltale dilating of the pupils.

Yet she was not giving him the come-on, either. That was clear too.

His brows drew together. How would she react to his next move? he wondered. He clicked on to the internet and made a rapid search, made a purchase online, clicking on 'deliver before noon'. Then, job done, he cleared the screen and put his mind into work mode. There was a lot to get done if he wanted to be free by the evening.

* * *

Marisa was hand-washing one of her beautiful new sweaters when the intercom rang. Frowning, she picked up the phone.

'Delivery for Ms Milburne,' said a disembodied voice.

Puzzled, she went downstairs. As she walked out into the lobby and saw a man standing on the pavement with a bouquet of white lilies she smiled. *Oh, Ian,* she thought fondly, *how sweet. Just because you couldn't meet me last night.*

But when she took the beautiful bouquet into her kitchen to find a suitable receptacle for it, and opened the small gilt-edged envelope attached to the wrapping, the card inside held an unexpected message.

Thank you for the milk and coffee—it was much appreciated.

It was simply signed 'Your grateful neighbour.'

For a moment she stared. As a token of gratitude a bouquet of lilies that must have cost at least thirty pounds, if not more, was a bit overdone. On the other hand...well, since being with Ian she had come to realise that the rich really were different. Anyone who could afford the rents on these apartments could definitely afford to drop thirty pounds on a bunch of flowers without even noticing.

Yet for all her rationalising, as she arranged the glorious blooms with their intense, heady fragrance in a huge glass vase she'd found in a cupboard, she could not help wishing they *had* been from Ian.

Not some stranger who meant absolutely nothing to her.

However much of an impact he'd made on her.

She'd been doing her best to put the incident last night out of her head. Dwelling on it was stupid. So was moping. She'd definitely started to mope yesterday, and it was time to nip that in the bud. Of *course* Ian found it hard to meet her—she knew why and accepted it, even if she wished it otherwise. Well, it wasn't otherwise, and that was that. And if she were feeling lonely without him—well, considering the luxury of her life now, it was ungrateful and spoilt to be anything other than blissful.

Doing the hand-washing helped improve her mood, and so did a resolve to go for a brisk walk in Holland Park. The weather wasn't attractive—mizzling with rain today—but that wasn't the point. She should get out, breathe fresh air— even if London air could never really be fresh—and get some exercise.

I ought to find a gym, or take some dance classes of some kind.

That would definitely be a good idea. She would ask in some of the shops on Holland Park Road when she went to buy groceries. If she did start exercise classes it might be a way of meeting people—other women she could chat to, have coffee with. Make friends with, maybe.

She wasn't very good at making friends, she knew. It was because she'd always felt different, felt out of things. Though she and her mother had lived in their small village off Dartmoor they hadn't really belonged—they'd always been incomers. Outsiders. And her mother's introverted temperament, and circumstance of being a single mother, had added to their social isolation. Even as school Marisa had always felt remote from her peer group, finding it difficult to make friends, get on with others. She felt a little glow start up inside her. That was why it was so lovely being with Ian. They got on so well. His charm, his sense of humour, his liveliness— all drew her out of herself, made her feel relaxed and confident for the first time in her life.

It made it all the more frustrating that she had to be a secret part of his life.

If only he could acknowledge me openly—not keep me tucked away here...

Yes, well, that was impossible. No point going over it again. No point starting to mope.

Grabbing her jacket, and slipping a waterproof around her, she picked up her keys and set off for a walk. She'd find a café and have some lunch, then pick up some shopping. That would pass the time.

Guilt plucked at her. *Pass the time.* Was that what she was doing with her life now? Finding things to do to while away the hours?

As she walked along the park's pathways, heading vaguely towards the remains of Holland House and the beautiful glass Orangery, she started to think critically. Wonderful as it was to live in so beautiful a flat, with no money worries and a life of luxury that she'd never dreamt of, she could *not* live her life like that.

She should find another job, she knew—but doing what? Ian had insisted she give up the low-paid cleaning jobs she'd been doing when she'd met him. A thought struck her, and she stopped and stared at a leafless bush dripping water droplets along its branches. Why not take up some kind of charity work? Since Ian was insisting on paying her bills, why not take advantage of not having to earn a living by doing something to help others? What, precisely, she had no idea, but she could make a start, surely, by finding one of the many charity shops and volunteering her time—sorting out donated goods or working at the till. The charity shop could probably show her other pieces that needed volunteers, and she could take it from there.

Resolution filled her, and she could feel her spirits lift. Her mind ran on, wondering where the nearest charity shops were likely to be. Somewhere up at Notting Hill, probably, or down on Kensington High Street. And there would definitely be some around Shepherds Bush Green, surely?

She would start checking after lunch. She'd use her new laptop and the apartment's built-in broadband to search, and then start phoning round to see what was available. With a reviving sense of enthusiasm she headed back to her flat. As she walked in she was hit by an exotic fragrance—it was the bouquet of lilies, giving off their wonderful scent, filling the living room with it. As it caught her nostrils she had a vivid recollection of the man who'd sent them.

He really was extraordinarily good-looking…

When the doorbell sounded just after six she jumped. She'd been doing a web search of charities, had got immersed in reading about the work done by them, and the time had flown by. Reading about just how terrible some people's lives were had been a timely, sobering reminder. Yes, her life had had its challenges, no doubt about that, and every day she missed her mother, but what they'd been through had been nothing compared with the sufferings of so many in the world. It had certainly served to squash any resumption of her moping and self-pity because she could see so little of Ian.

The doorbell sounded again. With a mix of slight apprehension, slight irritation at being disturbed, and slight curiosity as to who it might be, she went to open the door.

'Did the flowers arrive?'

The deep, accented voice did exactly to her insides what it had done the night before. So did the six-foot frame and the incredible looks and the way his dark eyes were resting on her…

She took a breath. It seemed very slightly strangulated, much to her annoyance.

'Yes. Thank you. Though they were completely unnecessary.' Her voice sounded staccato. Even brusque. She didn't want to appear rude, but on the other hand there was no way she was going to be all over him for his over-the-top gesture of thanks for her very slight gesture of neighbourliness.

He seemed unrebuffed by her response.

'Not at all,' he contradicted her.

That faint smile was quirking at his mouth and doing,

just as his voice and his looks had, what it had done to her yesterday.

'The kindness of strangers should never go unappreciated.' His eyes glinted with a hint of humour in their dark, gold-flecked depths. 'You've no idea how badly I needed some coffee. It just never dawned on me that although these apartments come furnished there wouldn't actually be any provisions in stock unless they'd been ordered beforehand.' He paused. 'Tell me,' he went on, and now there was a quizzical enquiry in his voice, 'have you succeeded in getting your coffee machine to obey you yet?'

Marisa swallowed. She knew exactly what she should do. She should say, *No, and it doesn't matter, thank you very much. Thank you for the flowers, but they really were quite unnecessary, I promise you.* And then, politely but firmly, she should wish him good evening and close the door.

That was definitely what she should do. Anything else was madness. Asking for trouble. For complications. For something that she could do without and what was more to the point *should* do without.

I don't need a tall, dark, handsome stranger in my life! And certainly not this one!

A little chill went through her. Besides, he could be anyone. Just because he wore a cashmere overcoat and a bespoke suit and Italian shoes, and lived in a luxury apartment, it didn't mean that he wasn't a serial killer...

Yet even as she entertained the possibility she knew it must surely be impossible. Whatever serial killers looked like, it was not someone who quite obviously spent most of his day ordering minions around and doubtless cutting deals with a string of zeroes in them.

Had he read the disquiet in her eyes? Interpreted her momentary hesitation as understandable reluctance to engage in conversation on her doorstep with a man she didn't know? He must have, because before she could answer him he started speaking again.

'I apologise,' he said. 'I'm being intrusive, and presuming on far too slight an acquaintance.'

If he hadn't apologised she might well have made the answer to him that as she'd intended—she really might, she thought distractedly. But there was something about the open apology, the air of quizzical ruefulness, the slight backing off and withdrawal she sensed in his body language, that stopped her. Or was it, she thought with a kind of hollowing inside her stomach, the way those gold-flecked eyes were resting on her? As if they could reach deep inside her, hold her mesmerised until she gazed back at him.

'No, not at all,' she said awkwardly. She sounded very English, very stilted, she knew. 'It was kind of you to offer to help with the coffee machine. But instant coffee is absolutely fine, and anyway I drink tea mostly.'

Oh, Lord, she thought, why on earth had she said that? Why had she spoken at all? Why hadn't she just smiled and shut the door. Why—?

'Quite right. Just what an English rose *should* drink,' he replied.

And now, completely openly, there was amusement in his voice. It did even more to her than his accent did.

'We Greeks, however,' he went on, 'drink our coffee like mud. A legacy from our Turkish overlords.'

'So you *are* Greek!'

The words fell from her lips before she could stop them.

The glint came again. 'Is that good or bad?' he said, humour clear in his voice.

'I don't know,' she said candidly. 'I don't know anyone who is Greek, and I've never been to Greece.'

His eyes glinted again. 'Well, I hope I will put you off neither my compatriots, nor my country,' he responded, with humour still in his voice, that smile in his eyes.

Marisa swallowed. No, whoever this guy was, he definitely did not put her off either Greeks or Greece...

He was speaking again, she realised with a start, and made herself pay attention.

'Having asked one favour of you already,' he was saying, and his eyes were washing over her again, to the same devastating effect, 'I am going to push my luck and ask another.' He paused and looked down at her, a look of speculative questioning in his expression. 'Are you at all interested in the theatre? I've come into possession of two tickets for a preview performance tonight of the Chekov that's opening next week. Can I persuade you to keep me company?'

He was taking a gamble here. Athan knew that. Chekov might be the last thing to persuade her. But his surveillance records indicated that she had spent numerous evenings at the theatre, and that included any number of high brow plays. Tickets for the upcoming Chekov were like gold dust, and might be sufficient temptation for her.

Marisa could only stand there. Her heart rate seemed to have quickened, and thoughts were racing through her head.

He's trying to pick me up—he's definitely trying to pick me up. Asking me to the theatre is a pick-up—no question about it! No ambiguity or misunderstanding like it was about the coffee machine—just a plain straightforward date to go to the theatre together...

A strange kind of thrill went through her, but there was a tremor in it too. Thanks to the remoteness of her childhood home, the difficulties of her upbringing with her lonely, isolated mother, she had little experience of men. She knew she had the kind of looks they liked, but her mother had considered her beauty more of a danger than a blessing—just as her mother's looks had proved a danger to her when she'd been young, Marisa thought sadly. It had taken Ian's open admiration for her to let her blossom finally. His insistence that she indulge herself in beautiful clothes and lavish beauty treatments had finally convinced her that it was OK for men to find her attractive.

Even, she accepted, with another little thrill, this devastatingly gorgeous man, standing here inviting her out for the evening.

Of course it was unquestionably out of the question. It had to be. She couldn't go on a date with a strange man just because he happened to live—very temporarily—next door to her. Good grief, she didn't even know his name. Only that he was rich. And Greek.

And irresistibly good-looking…

And that combination makes a male that assumes he's going to get his own way, my girl! So you know perfectly well what you're going to say, don't you? You're going to smile, a small, tight little smile and step backwards, to convey the right body language, then say, politely but adamantly, No, thank you. And you are going to close the door and not have anything more to do with him. That's what you're going to do.

She opened her mouth to do just that. Which meant that it was incredibly, unbelievably annoying when what she heard her voice saying was, 'Is that that new production of *Three Sisters* that I've read about in the papers?'

'That's the one. Would you be interested?'

Marisa swallowed. Yes, she would be interested. Anyone who loved the theatre would be. She'd seen it advertised and it had a stellar cast, including a Hollywood star keen to make her mark as a classical actress.

But was that any reason to accept what this complete stranger had just offered?

She must have made her hesitation apparent, because before she could say anything more, he spoke again.

'Perhaps,' he said, and his voice had changed slightly, as had the expression in his eyes, though she wasn't entirely sure how, 'it might be timely at this juncture to reassure you that I am not, as you may possibly be currently wondering,

either a murderer, a burglar, a spy or wanted for questioning
by Interpol. I am, for my pains, merely a businessman, and
tediously respectable...'

There was a mix of humour and frankness in his voice,
and as he spoke he reached a long-fingered hand inside his
jacket pocket and withdrew a silver card case, flicking it
open and withdrawing one of its contents, proffering it to her
with another of those quick, quirking smiles that seemed to
have such a powerful effect on her in disproportion to their
duration.

She found herself taking the card, staring at it. It was written in Latin script and it said simply, 'Teodarkis Holdings'.
There was a Mayfair address, and a discreet name in the
corner: Athan Teodarkis.

Athan watched her peruse the card. There was a lot rid-
ing on her reaction. A whole, game-changing lot. He was
taking the gamble that Ian had never mentioned the name of
his wife's family to her, or the company that owned the one
he worked for himself. As he studied her face he could see
nothing that would indicate, even under high-focus scrutiny,
that it meant anything to her at all. He could feel relief rippling through him.

He gave her a moment or two to study the business card,
then addressed her again.

'Does that convince you I am totally harmless?' he asked.

There was a touch of light humour in his voice, and she let
her eyes glance up at him from the white card in her fingers.

Harmless? The word reverberated in her head. *Harmless?*
As she looked straight at him, at his breathtaking dark good-
looks, the word seemed to mock her.

'So,' he was saying, 'will you come? I hate going to the
theatre on my own.'

'Surely there must be someone you already know that you
could invite?' she countered. There was just a trace of acid-
ity in her voice, because a man like this, who was the very

last man any female would ever describe as 'harmless', must
have a very long list of women who would drop everything
for a date with him.

'No one who likes Chekov,' he responded promptly. 'He's
not to everyone's taste.'

Hmm, thought Marisa, for not 'everyone' read 'the kind
of high-maintenance glossy woman whose idea of a hot date
with a man like him would *not* be a play by a nineteenth century Russian dramatist about a bunch of gloomy, indecisive
provincials who drifted about aimlessly and got depressed'.

'And you think I would?' she challenged, suddenly and
illogically stung that he clearly did not consider *her* the kind
of female he usually asked out. 'Is that your reason for asking me?' she said pointedly.

Long lashes dipped down over gold-flecked eyes. 'Part
of it,' he agreed.

The dark eyes rested on her, conveying their message. A
message that told her that whatever she might have thought
about not being the kind of woman he usually asked out, she
had, in fact, been mistaken...

There was something new in his voice—something that
told Marisa this was a very experienced operator indeed. For
a second panic beat in her throat. She was out of her depth—
way, way out! Oh, he might be seeing a woman living in a
luxury apartment, dressed in designer clothes and looking
svelte and groomed, but she knew that beneath that glossy
surface she was only a raw country girl. Even her short time
with Ian couldn't eradicate that.

She suddenly realised he was speaking again.

'Well—have I persuaded you?' There was nothing more
than the familiar quizzical enquiry in his voice, his expression.

Marisa swallowed. 'Um...I—I...'

He smiled. The full on smile that changed his face, turned
her insides out, parted her lips and made her stare gormlessly
at him.

'Great. OK—so, can you be ready by seven?'

'Um—'

'Good girl,' he said approvingly, as if she'd agreed to his invitation. He made as if to step away, then suddenly paused, as if something had just struck him. 'I've just realised,' he said, and there was self-reproof in his voice, 'I've absolutely no idea what your name is.'

He made the omission sound like a cause for humour, not an indication that she was a complete stranger to him. He looked at her expectantly.

There was a strange sensation in Marisa's head. As if everything that was going on was completely, totally unreal. Then, as if in a haze, she said slowly, 'It's Marisa— Marisa Milburne.'

The long lashes swept down again. Then, before she had the faintest inkling of what he was about to do, she felt, of all things, her hand being taken, and lifted.

'I'm delighted to make your acquaintance, Miss Milburne,' he murmured, holding her wide-eyed gaze.

Instantly she held her breath, and he inclined his head and kissed her hand.

It was fleeting, it was momentary, it was over in a second, but it left her bereft of rationality.

'To compensate for the informality of our acquaintance,' he murmured.

Then, with a final stomach-dissolving smile, he turned and headed down to the lift. Marisa stared, incapable of movement, until the doors had opened, then closed again, shutting him off from her view. Then, very slowly, in a total daze, she went back into her apartment.

Inside, she stood, staring at her hand for several seconds, bereft of both speech and all rational thought.

Least of all any sense of danger…

CHAPTER TWO

'WELL, what do you think? Should she stick to Hollywood?'

The curtain had fallen, and Marisa was making her slow way out of the stalls. Athan Teodarkis's tall presence behind her was almost tangible as he followed her. But then it had been tangible the entire evening. Tangible even when he'd been on the far side of a taxi seat from her on the way to the theatre, let alone when he'd been sitting right next to her in the plush stalls seat, his sleeve almost brushing hers, even though she'd tried to make sure she kept her hands in her lap, not resting on the chair arm like he had.

A hundred times she'd told herself that she should never have accepted his invitation. That it was completely unacceptable to have done so, and a big, big mistake.

She didn't know the man. Didn't know him from Adam. However prestigious a business card he possessed, he was a stranger—a stranger who had quite blatantly picked her up. Not quite off the street, but even so—being some random guy in the flat next to hers was not exactly a formal introduction, was it? But the moment she thought about the total absence of any kind of formal introduction the memory of that hand-kiss was there, and the fleeting sensation of his lips scarcely brushing her knuckles...

No wonder Victorian maidens swooned when men kissed their hands!

How, she wondered for the millionth time, could such a formal gesture be so incredibly...*intimate*? For intimate was the only word for it. And swooning the only word for the sensation it had created....

The sensation that permeated her still. Not quite as intense, but there all the same, like a very low-level fever that had been running in her veins constantly, all evening. She'd sought to ignore it, sought to make herself behave with this man as if he *weren't* having that effect on her, as if it were perfectly normal to make polite, anodyne conversation about the play, the theatre, the state of London traffic, sounding composed and unaffected and sensible.

She'd deliberately dressed in a style that was demure— there was no better word for it. No way was she going to give him the slightest reason to think she was coming on to him! Either by her manner or her appearance. So the grey light wool dress she'd chosen was smart, no doubt about that, and had a mid-range designer tag, but the neckline was not low and the cut was quite loose, its hemline touching her knee. Matching grey tights and grey low-heeled shoes went with it, and the only jewellery she wore was a metallic haematite necklace. Her hair was dressed in a plaited coil at the back of her head, and her make up was as discreet as the rest of her.

Had he looked very slightly surprised at the overall demureness of her appearance? She wasn't sure, but if he had the look had disappeared immediately, and his manner towards her had mirrored her own. He was courteous and conversational, but he was not coming on to her—to her relief.

It *was* to her relief, wasn't it? She was *glad* he was simply talking to her as if she were, say, the wife of a friend or a colleague, or even a middle-aged woman. Because of course she wouldn't want him to talk to her as if she were a female he found attractive or wanted to make up to, would she?

Of course not, she told herself firmly. So, keeping that clear in her mind, she answered now, as they made their way into the foyer, 'I thought she was pretty good all round. At first I kept only seeing her as a "star," but after a while I just saw her as her character, and I thought she did it better than one might have expected.'

'Interesting,' he commented, 'that she took the role of the oldest and dowdiest sister—when her Hollywood parts are always so glamorous.'

'I expect she thought it was the most challenging part,' she answered lightly. 'Playing against type.'

His response was 'Yes, very probably,' and then he made a comment about another of the cast. As they walked out onto the pavement, the chilly air hitting her, he guided her towards the left.

'I do hope,' she heard him say, 'that you will agree to having a post-theatre dinner with me? I find that an evening performance is never best timed to eat either before or after.'

She felt her arm being taken. Not in a possessive way, let alone in any kind of intimate way, but simply lightly, cupping her elbow to guide her along the pavement. Guiding her where he wanted her to go.

For a moment she felt she ought to refuse, then she gave a mental shrug. She was hungry, and since she'd already gone to the theatre with him what harm would there be in going on to a restaurant? Besides, she wanted to talk about the play, and if she just went home there would be no one to talk to.

There never was, apart from Ian.

A pang went through her but she thrust it aside. She was lucky—beyond lucky!—to have Ian in her life now, and as for making friends in London—well, that was entirely up to her. She would volunteer for a charity, start up exercise classes, possibly evening classes as well—why not? And she'd soon have friends here—of course she could. She had a brand-new life, courtesy of Ian, and she would make the very most of it.

The restaurant Athan Teodarkis took her to was only a short walk from the theatre. It wasn't, she was glad to see, either a very crowded, popular one, or a quiet, intimate one. There were a fair number of other diners there, but the lighting was not conducive to romantic dining *à deux*, and she felt reassured. Post-theatre seduction was evidently *not*, thank goodness, on her escort's mind.

All that *was* on his mind, it seemed, was ordering from the menu, choosing wine, and then being perfectly prepared to discuss the production they'd just seen.

'I have to admit,' he opined, having nodded to the sommelier to fill their glasses and taken an appreciative mouthful of the wine, 'that the play did irritate me in respect of the sisters' endless preoccupation with wanting to go to Moscow but never going. I kept finding myself wanting to shout *Just buy a train ticket!*'

Marisa gave the requisite smile in response, but then said ruminatively, 'But if you're not used to travel, and you've always lived in one place, then going to a big city can be very daunting.'

Athan's eyes rested on her a moment. 'You sound like you speak from experience?'

'Well, yes, I do. Up until recently I'd never left Devon. It sounds odd, in this day and age, but I'd never been to London.' It was an admission she suddenly felt unsure about making, as if revealing it might put him off her. But it didn't seem to.

'What made you come here?' His voice was neutral.

She gave a little shrug. 'Oh, wanting to see the bright lights and so on. Usual reasons, really.'

The nonchalance in her voice did not deceive him. Yet he found himself unable to decide what was the cause of it. On the most cynical interpretation it could be, a blithe glossing over of an ambition to come up to London and catch the attention of a wealthy man…just as she had with his brother-in-law. But he had to acknowledge it might also be, simply because she felt that being seen as a country girl didn't go with her sophisticated image.

Not that she was presenting a sophisticated image tonight, he also had to acknowledge. He'd been unable to suppress a flicker of slight surprise when he'd first set eyes on her and taken in her outfit for the evening. *Demure* had been the word that came to his mind, and it was an odd one for a female who was happy for a married man to lavish his money on her.

Once again he felt a flicker of emotion go through him. He was glad she hadn't taken the opportunity to dress to kill this evening, to attempt openly to wow him. Instead, the fact that she was playing down her natural beauty was, he realised, really quite appealing…

He made another comment about the performance, drawing another response in kind from her, and by the time their first course arrived he was aware that he was, against his expectations, enjoying talking to her. Her views were intelligent and informed, and she revealed a sensitivity to the play's characters' various dilemmas that showed she understood the complexities of their situations—even that of the sisters' feckless brother.

'I suppose the brother is the least sympathetic character,' she was saying, 'though I suppose one has to allow that he made a disastrous marriage and make some excuses for him.'

Athan stilled. 'Does an unhappy marriage excuse bad behaviour?' He knew there was nothing audible in his voice other than dispassionate enquiry. His mouth, however, had tightened. However insightful she might be about Chekov, it didn't blind him to the fact that she was still in the dock about the way she chose to live her private life.

'Sometimes, perhaps,' Marisa said slowly. 'The second sister, Masha, wouldn't have had an affair if she'd been happily married, would she?'

'And that exonerates her, does it?'

Now the edge was audible in his voice, and Marisa looked across at him.

'I think it depends on each individual situation,' she said.

There was a shadow in her eyes as she spoke, and Athan did not miss it.

So, was that what she was telling herself? he thought. That Ian Randall was unhappily married, so that gave him—and her—*carte blanche* to have an affair?

'Do you think Masha's husband was right to forgive her?' His question was blunt.

'Well, divorce was probably impossible in those days, wasn't it? He would just have to make the best of things, I guess.'

Athan reached for his wine. 'Ah, yes, divorce—a very convenient option.'

Marisa looked at him. 'But not one that's always taken,' she said.

She looked away again. This wasn't a subject she wanted to discuss. It was too close, too painful, and the arrival of their main course was a welcome interruption.

As the waiters departed she picked up her knife and fork and said, deliberately seeking a new topic, 'What brings *you* to London?'

Her voice was bright and enquiring. Glancing at her, realising she was deliberately steering him away from a subject that was obviously too close to the bone for her, Athan momentarily wondered how she would react if he told her the truth: *I'm here to stop you having an adulterous affair with Ian Randall...my brother-in-law.*

Instead, of course, he responded in a similar vein to her conversational opening.

'Unlike the three sisters, I travel extensively for my work. I'm primarily based in Athens, but the company is international and travel goes with the ticket.'

A wistful look entered her eyes. 'That must be wonderful,' she said.

He gave a mordant smile. 'It can get tedious,' he answered.

'One airport is very much like another in the end—and offices are very similar wherever in the world they are.'

'Yes, I suppose it palls after a while.'

He looked at her speculatively. 'Why don't you try it some time—travel? If you'll excuse me saying so, you have the means to do so, don't you?'

Living in a Holland Park flat as she did, wearing the expensive closthes she did, it was a reasonable assumption for him to make—assuming, of course, he didn't know that she was *not* a free agent and that her accommodation and wardrobe were provided by a lover who was London-based and would want to keep his mistress close by and not gadding about abroad.

Her response confirmed that assessment of her situation.

A hesitant expression flitted across her face. 'Oh, it would be a bit difficult at the moment. But, yes, perhaps one day—it would be wonderful to see other countries.'

'What would be your first choice?' he asked. An idea was forming in his mind, but he needed more information first.

She glanced out of the window at the wintry rain that had started to descend through the streetlights.

'Anywhere with a tropical beach!' she said with a laugh.

He gave a light, answering laugh. 'Yes, I can see the appeal.'

She looked at him. 'You must be used to hot weather?'

'Contrary to popular opinion, Athens can have very cold weather sometimes,' he said wryly. 'At this time of year you'd need to go a lot further south to find any warmth, let alone tropical beaches.'

Even as he spoke his mind was racing ahead. Would it be feasible, what he'd just thought of? It would take some reorganisation, but it could certainly be done. Best of all, a cold, cynical part of his brain told him, it would be something she could not lie about afterwards. If he had to he could demonstrably prove to Ian that the woman he wanted to make his mistress had preferred another man to him.

She was speaking again, saying something about dream holiday destinations, and he turned his attention back to her. Her expression was more animated now, as if she were losing the guard that she'd put up against him all evening.

Was it deliberate, this lightening up, or was she unconscious of it?

Whichever it is, animation only makes her yet more beautiful.

As she spoke his gaze rested on her. Sitting across a dining table from her like this, he could see exactly why Ian Randall was so smitten with her. She could have been wearing a sack, for all her appearance was seeking to mute her beauty. Hers was a beauty that shone like a star.

Can I really go through with this?

The unwelcome question uncoiled again in his mind, troubling him. It had seemed easy enough when he'd decided this was the best, fastest and most irreversible way of terminating her relationship with Ian. But now that he was only a few feet away from her, dining with her, talking with her...drinking in her blonde, perfect beauty...was it really such a good idea? Were there hidden dangers that he did not see ahead of him?

He pushed the thought aside ruthlessly. Of course there was no danger—not to him. He would do what he intended, achieve what he'd set out to do, and then walk away, his purpose accomplished. Unscathed. Of course unscathed.

Why would he even be thinking of anything else?

Not the way her cheekbones seem to be sculpted out of alabaster, or the blue of her eyes seems to catch the reflection of a tranquil sea, or her mouth seems as tender as a newly ripe peach...

He tore his mind away from cataloguing her physical attributes and back to what she was talking about. He realised he had no idea what she'd just said.

'I'm sorry—you were saying...?' he said.

She seemed to have faltered to a stop, and he wondered

at it. Then he realised she was simply looking at him. A faint colour was staining her cheekbones—*those cheekbones carved from alabaster*, he thought, then pushed it aside. Her eyelashes swept down over her eyes, veiling their expression. But it was too late—he'd seen it, recognised it...

Knew it for what it was.

Marisa felt heat flare in her face, dipped her gaze swiftly. But she knew it was too late. Knew that she hadn't been able to disguise her reaction to the way he'd just been looking at her. The power of his gaze, the message clear and unambiguous in his eyes. She felt hot, then shivery, as if one moment her blood was heating in her veins, and the next it had drained from her, pooling somewhere very deep inside her. She felt a breathlessness, a constriction in her throat, a hectic beating of her heart.

She fought for composure. It wasn't supposed to happen! This wasn't supposed to be anything like this. She was here with him only because he'd invited her to the theatre, then to dinner afterwards—it wasn't a date, not in the romance sense. Of course it wasn't!

He's a stranger! I don't know him!

But she knew enough.

Enough to tell her that when he looked at her he was looking at her not as someone to accompany him to a play or to talk to him about it afterwards.

All that stuff she'd told herself about how he was behaving like she was the wife of a friend, or a colleague, or a middle aged woman...it mocked her—made a fool of her self-pretence.

Jerkily, she got on with eating. That was what she must do—focus on the meal, on getting to the end of it. Making herself chit-chat about anything and nothing—it didn't really matter what.

And don't look at him—not like that. Ignore him—make myself ignore him—if he looks at me.

It took self-discipline and effort—a lot of effort—but she managed to stick to her resolve. For the rest of the meal she made light, bright conversation, doggedly not meeting his eyes, not gazing at him, not paying any attention at all to the way his eyes seemed to be flecked with gold, or the way lines formed around his mouth when he smiled, or the way his head turned, the way his strong, long-fingered hands curved around the stem of his wine glass, or the way his deep, accented voice played on her nerve-endings like the low bass notes of a song that pulsed slow and heavy in her veins...

But it was as if there were two of her. One that was doing the light, bright chit-chat and another, watching from inside, wanting to do what she was not allowing herself to do. To drink him in, feel the power of his physicality, his presence, his impact on her.

In the taxi back to Holland Park she was as jittery as a cat, sliding to the far side of the seat, deliberately putting her handbag down beside her, as if to form a barricade against him, and then leaping out of the cab as fast as she could when they alighted. She kept up the hectic, inconsequential chatter as they ascended in the lift, ignoring—doggedly ignoring!—the fact that they were enclosed in a small, six-by-six box with no one else, alone together, and the moment the lift doors opened she was out in the corridor and turning towards him.

'Thank you so much for a lovely evening,' she said, in the light, bright voice she had kept up so determinedly. 'It was so kind of you—I really enjoyed myself.' She put a bright social smile on her face. 'Goodnight,' she said airily.

Athan looked down at her. OK, so she was holding him off. Keeping him at bay. Well, he would go along with it—for now.

He gave her the faint half-smile he'd used before. 'Goodnight, Marisa—I'm glad you enjoyed yourself. So did I.'

There was nothing in his voice or his expression to show her that he was playing along with her, but he was sure he saw her colour deepen fractionally before she turned away and got her key out of her bag to open her front door. Did she fumble slightly as she did so? And was that for the reason he wanted it to be? He watched her open the door and step inside, her hand lifting in a little half-wave of farewell as she shut the door on him.

For a moment or two he stood looking at her closed apartment door, his own face closed as well. Eyes masked. Thoughts went through his head. Conflicting, disturbing thoughts that were a waste of his time. That interfered with his purpose.

Then, with an abrupt turn on his heel, he strode down to his own apartment, and went inside.

He had made it to first base with her, just as he'd planned. Now it was a question of taking it to the next stage.

The idea he'd had during dinner flared again in his head. It was attractive, simple, decisive—and it would sever her, unquestionably from Ian Randall, in the shortest possible time.

He was quite some distance from it yet—there was more preparation to do. A lot more. But when it was complete Marisa Milburne would never be available to his brother-in-law again.

'Aren't you going to open it?'

Athan's voice held its familiar note of faint amusement as she stared down at the envelope he'd placed in front of her at their table in the restaurant. Marisa knew that tone of voice by now. It made him sound as if he found her behaviour funny but he chose to indulge it. Chose to indulge the way she behaved with him.

As if what was happening wasn't happening at all. As if she hadn't for the past two weeks held him at arm's length. Not that he'd tried to close the distance. She had to allow him that—and be appreciative of it. Of course if he *had* tried to close the distance she would have bolted instantly. Of course she would! If he'd made a move on her, flirted with her, come on to her, she'd have backed away—retreated out of reach.

But he hadn't. For a start, for several days after their theatre date she hadn't even set eyes on him. Well, that was understandable. It had been the weekend, and he'd probably gone back to Athens. Or spent his time with someone else.

Who else?

The moment she'd asked the question, she had supplied the answer. A woman, of course—someone svelte, glamorous and gorgeous. A supermodel, a high-powered career woman, a glittering socialite...her mind had run through the possibilities. Not someone like her—a quiet, provincial girl who didn't move in the kind of circles a man like him would move in. She was someone he'd taken to the theatre on the spur of the moment because he'd had no one else to take to such a play, and that was all. Not that she was asking for more—of course she wasn't. But it was as well to face the facts—a female who lived on her own, didn't go out anywhere, and was new to London didn't usually get to hang out with sinfully good-looking Greek tycoons.

The theatre date had been a one-off. That was the obvious conclusion. And the one she'd wanted. Hadn't she? Of course she had—hadn't she spent the whole evening reminding herself he was a complete stranger?

Except when she'd got back home in her flat again she'd realised she'd enjoyed the evening. Not just because it had been so nice to go to the theatre with someone else, but because his company had been so good. Oh, not only because he was so ludicrously good looking, but because it had been interesting to talk to him, to exchange views on the play with him. It had been mentally stimulating, and the discussion they'd had still buzzed in her head.

Spending that weekend on her own—she had accepted she could never see Ian at the weekends, for that was the time he spent with his wife—had brought home to her just how isolated she felt here in London, however easy and luxurious her life. Her resolve to get some sort of voluntary work, try and make friends, had strengthened, and on the Monday she'd headed for the nearest charity shop and enquired about volunteering. Then she'd investigated dance classes nearby, and signed up for those as well. But her good mood had been dashed later that day, when Ian had phoned. Yet again he wouldn't be able to meet her. He hadn't even known when he could be free to see her again—maybe later that week, maybe not.

He'd been apologetic, she'd been understanding. Of course she had. His job was demanding, especially at the moment, and there were a lot more demands on his time than work—including from his wife. That was understandable. It was all understandable.

But as he'd rung off, having cancelled yet another lunchtime with her, she'd felt depression pluck at her. When the phone had rung again, a little while later, and a deep accented voice had spoken, she'd felt her spirits lift in reaction.

'This is completely on the off chance,' Athan Teodarkis's distinctively accented voice had said, 'but would you have any interest in seeing *Hamlet* at the National? Or have you already been?'

'I'd love to!' she said immediately.

His voice warmed. 'Excellent. Would Thursday suit?'

For a moment Marisa hesitated. Thursday was usually the evening that Ian was able to meet her without arousing his wife's suspicions. Eva went to her book club that day and wouldn't be aware he'd returned late, or would accept that he'd just been at the office. But his phone call earlier had already warned her that this week he really would be stuck at the office, burning the midnight oil on a complex deal he was closely involved with.

He'll probably be relieved if I make another arrange-

ment. He won't feel bad about not being able to see me, she reasoned.

A second later she gave Athan Teodarkis his answer.

The answer he wanted, the answer he'd intended to extract from her. He'd deliberately let her cool her heels over the weekend, knowing that Ian Randall never saw her at that time. For once—Athan's lip curled—he'd be playing the devoted husband.

But with the weekend over he'd known he needed to target Marisa Milburne again, and continue with his strategy to part her from her married swain.

As with the Chekov, *Hamlet* was followed by dinner, over which their discussion of the production predominated. Yet again Marisa made sure she was wearing the kind of outfit that wouldn't scream *Find me attractive!* and yet again Athan Teodarkis behaved scrupulously towards her, bidding her a chaste goodnight at her door once again.

Expecting another solitary weekend, Marisa was surprised when her doorbell sounded just before midday the following Sunday

'It's a glorious sunny day—can I persuade you to lunch at the Belvedere in Holland Park?' Athan Teodarkis invited.

Her face lit. 'Oh, that sounds wonderful! I've never been there.'

He smiled—that increasingly familiar quirking of his well-shaped mouth. 'Then I must definitely take you. It's memorable.'

She took a breath. 'This time it's on me. I insist you must be my guest for a change.'

His expression stilled. For a moment Marisa thought she had offended him. Then, his eyes still veiled, he gave a distinct shake of his head.

'That's not in the least necessary,' he said, and there was a clipped note to his voice.

Marisa looked at him uncertainly. There seemed to be a

shadow in his eyes. She couldn't quite see into them. A little chill went through her.

Then it was gone. 'Cook me a meal one evening,' he said. 'Simple fare will do me fine. Oh, and I can show you how to work that coffee machine of yours!'

'OK,' she said slowly, not sure whether it was still that momentary chill that disturbed her, or the prospect of Athan Teodarkis coming into her apartment, eating dinner there...

Had she really felt that chill? she wondered later, as they set off for Holland Park.

Athan set a brisk pace and she kept up with it—walking was one thing, after her rural upbringing, where transport was sparse and the wilds of Dartmoor were close at hand, she had become inured her to. It was, as he had said, a glorious day—but very cold. She was glad of her pure wool jacket and warm leather boots as they walked through the park towards the restaurant, which was situated in the ballroom that was almost all that was left of the grand Holland House that had once stood there.

She wished she'd brought a pair of sunglasses, as Athan had. As she glanced sideways at him she could feel her insides do a little somersault. What was it about dark glasses that made him look so...so even *more* than he already looked in spades!

She snapped her head away. He was glancing down at her, she was sure of it, and being caught gazing at him was *not* what she wanted. Did his mouth give that familiar quirk? she wondered. To cover herself, she started talking. 'I do love Holland Park, even at this time of year. It's a real haven. I come here all the time. It's such a shame that Holland House itself got bombed in the war—all that's left is enough for a youth hostel. And the Orangery, where the Belvedere restaurant is, of course. Apparently there's an opera season in the summer. All outdoors. It must be wonderful on a warm summer's night!'

She was babbling, but she couldn't help it. He didn't seem to mind, though, and made an appropriate response to what she'd said, and they continued chatting as they made their way towards the restaurant.

The setting was indeed memorable—an eighteenth century summer ballroom, with beautiful long windows all around that let the winter sunshine pour in. And lunch was superb. Marisa wondered again whether to offer to pay, for she felt bad eating at his expense a third time, but found she dared not mention it again. He would take offence, she was sure. It was probably something he just wasn't used to. Even so, she felt she ought to insist, and it made her feel very slightly uncomfortable.

Apart from that, however, Marisa found she was the most comfortable yet in his company. He was, she realised with a little start, no longer a stranger...

She didn't know much about him personally—but then they weren't really talking about personal things. She was glad. She obviously couldn't discuss Ian, but she also didn't want to talk about her life in Devon. It was behind her now— she would not be going back. She felt a little flush go through her. Besides, Athan Teodarkis clearly saw her as a young woman of independent means, who lived in a plush apartment and wore expensive clothes. What would he think of her if he knew she'd been brought up in a run down cottage by an impoverished single mother who'd struggled to keep their heads above water?

But all that was a universe away from the way she lived now. She looked about her at the beautiful, expensive restaurant serving the most exquisite food, looked at the man she was lunching with, who headed up his own personal international company and casually talked about going to places in private jets and chauffeur-driven cars, and having an army of minions at his disposal. His sunglasses had a famous logo on them and his gold wristwatch was, she knew, a priceless heirloom. Athan Teodarkis had *rich* written all over him...

Sleek, assured, cosmopolitan, sophisticated.

Devastating...

A little thrill went through her. A susurration of awareness that of all the women in the world he could be choosing to spend his Sunday with it was her.

This was no one-off, no convenient using up of a theatre ticket. This was, she knew with a flutter of butterflies in her stomach, a genuine invitation to her personally. Because he wanted her company.

It was the only conclusion she could come to—and she came to the same conclusion over the following week, when he took her to a concert at the Royal Festival Hall and a production of *Twelfth Night*.

And invited himself to dinner at her flat.

She could hardly refuse, since she'd tacitly agreed that it was to be the way she would return all the dining out she'd done with him—not to mention the theatre tickets. Even so, she was very nervous. And not just because she had no idea what to cook that a man like him could possibly want to eat. Her culinary skills were entirely basic.

She admitted as much to his face, and was relieved when he smiled.

'Actually, I was hoping you might see your way to a traditional English roast,' he said.

'I think I can stretch to that,' she said, adding hopefully, 'How do you feel about apple crumble for pudding?' Along with roast dinners, pies and pastries were the one thing her mother had taught her.

'Crumble?' he quizzed.

'Pastry without water!' she exclaimed. 'Loads easier!'

So it proved—and so did the rest of the meal, including the company. She'd done her best to provide a traditional English roast, and he certainly seemed very appreciative of it. For herself, though, her stomach was full of butterflies—and not because she was worried the meal was not up to his standards.

It was because he was sitting at the dining table in her apartment and there was no one else around. Oh, she could tell herself all she liked that she was behaving with him no differently than if he hadn't been a drop-dead gorgeous male who raised her heart-rate just by quirking his half-smile at her, but she knew it wasn't true. Knew that for all her deliberately dressing in a cowl-necked jumper and jeans, with minimal make-up and her hair in a casual ponytail, she was all too aware that Athan Teodarkis was having a powerful impact on her.

Knew that she was having an increasingly hard time in keeping that awareness at bay, and was wondering just why she had to...

By strength of will she managed to get through to the end of the meal, keeping up a semblance of unresponsiveness to him, behaving outwardly as if he *weren't* having the kind of impact on her that he was. She wasn't sure just why she felt it was so vital to do so, only knew that it was.

I can't lower my guard—I just can't!

But it was getting harder—much, much harder.

Out in the kitchen after the apple crumble—which she'd served with custard and clotted cream and had had the satisfaction of seeing him polish off up, though just where it had gone on his lean, powerful frame she had no idea—he tackled the fearsome coffee machine, calling her over to explain the mechanism to her.

She was far too close to him. Far too close, his hand was pointing out the controls, his shoulders were almost brushing hers, his hip jutting against hers. His face was far too close as he turned to explain something to her. She jerked away, pulse leaping.

Had he noticed? Noticed the way she had drawn away and started to gabble something to cover her nerves? Something about how she loved cappuccino but hated espresso. She didn't think he had—or at any rate, he didn't show that he had, and that was what was important. That he didn't think she was getting ideas about him.

Flustered, she busied herself retrieving coffee cups from one of the cupboards and setting the tray. She carried the tray through and set it down on the coffee table, sat herself squarely on the armchair, leaving the whole expanse of the sofa opposite for him. No way was she going to let him think she wanted him up close and personal beside her.

Did he smile faintly as he saw where she'd sat herself? She wasn't sure and didn't want to think about it. Wanted only, as they drank coffee accompanied by music of her choice— some brisk, scintillating Vivaldi, definitely nothing soft and romantic—to get to a point where she could smother a yawn, thank him for coming and wait for him to take his leave.

Because that was what she wanted, wasn't it? Of course it was! Anything else was unthinkable—quite unthinkable. Unthinkable to covertly watch him drinking his coffee— rich and fragrant now that it was no longer instant—with one long leg crossed casually over another, his light blue cashmere sweater stretched across his chest so that she could almost discern the outline of his honed pecs and broad shoulders, his sable hair glinting in the lamplight, and the faintest dark shadow along his jawline that made her out of nowhere wonder what it would feel like to ease her fingertips along its chiselled line…

She blinked, horrified at herself.

This had to stop, right now! She mustn't start getting ideas—ideas that involved her and Athan Teodarkis up close and personal. The trouble was, that was exactly what was happening as they sat there, chatting about this and that, with him so obviously relaxed, like a cat that had dined well, and her curled up on the wide armchair opposite, with good red Burgundy coursing slowly through her veins and the low light from the table lamps, and the Vivaldi now changing to something a lot slower, more meditative and soothing...

Seductive...

He was looking at her, his dark, opaque eyes resting on her, with a veiled expression in them. Conversation seemed to have died away, desultory as it was, and Marisa tried to make a show of listening to the music.

Not looking at Athan.

Not taking in the way the light and shadow played with the planes of his features, the way his broad shoulders were moulding to the deep cushions of the sofa, or the way his long, jeans-clad legs seemed lean and lithe, how his fingers were curled around the coffee cup, shaping it as if they were cupping her face...

There was a knot inside her. A knot of intense feeling like a physical sensation. As if she couldn't move. Couldn't do anything except sit there, her hands splayed on the wide arms of the chair, her breathing shallow, her heart tumbling around inside her.

His eyes held hers, and her own eyes widened—dilated. Something changed in his. Flared with sudden light.

She jack-knifed to her feet.

'Oh, my goodness!' she exclaimed, her voice slightly too high-pitched. 'I...I think I left the oven on. I can't remember turning it off when I took out the apple crumble. What an idiot I am! I'd better go and check—'

She hurried out to the kitchen. She hadn't left the oven on. She knew she hadn't. But she'd had to break the moment. Had to stop what was starting to happen. Because...

Because—

Because if he stays...

But she mustn't think about what would happen if he stayed. Must only head back into the sitting room, smile brightly and say how late it was.

Which she did. And she stayed standing, making it pointedly obvious that she expected Athan to stand likewise. Which he did. But she was all too aware he did so with a kind of suppressed amusement, as if he knew perfectly well why she'd suddenly become so animated and hyper. He strolled towards the door, pausing when he got there. She trotted after him, mouthing politenesses which he replied to with an appropriate murmur. But when he turned back to her she could see, quite disastrously, that glint in his eye.

'Sleep well,' he said.

His voice was low, and his accent more pronounced. Or maybe she was just more sensitive to it.

'Yes. Thank you.' Her reply was staccato. More high pitched than her normal voice. She felt wired, with adrenaline coursing through her. Why didn't he go? Walk out the door?

Stop looking at her like that.

For one long, endless moment he seemed to be just letting his gaze rest on her. She couldn't tell what he was thinking— knew only that if it was what she thought he was thinking he could just *un*-think it. Because—well, just *because,* that was all.

She'd think about why afterwards. But not now. Definitely not now when, as if in slow motion, she saw his hand reach out towards her, felt his fingers graze her cheek, so lightly, so incredibly and devastatingly lightly. It was a moment only— scarcely there, hardly enough time to register it. But it made her skin glow, and even after his hand had dropped away it was as if he was still touching her.

He smiled. A deep, amused smile. Still holding her helpless gaze.

Almost she went to him—almost she took that tiny fatal half-step towards him. She knew with absolute, searing certainty that he would draw her to him and lower his mouth to hers…

Almost—

But not quite.

Summoning all her failing strength, she stepped away. 'Goodnight,' she said.

Long lashes swept down over his eyes, veiling his regard. The glint was gone. Vanished. 'Goodnight,' he answered. His voice was nothing more than polite now—cool, even. Then, with a brief nod of his head, he was gone.

Outside in the corridor, with her apartment door firmly shut, he strode down towards his own flat. His face was closed. Troubled.

He wanted her. He knew that. Impossible to deny it. He desired the beautiful, demurely alluring woman who was Marisa Milburne. Desired her whether or not she was anything at all to do with his brother-in-law's lamentable weakness of character.

Oh, he'd known from the first moment of seeing her photo that it would be no hardship to him to seduce her for his own purposes. But with every encounter with her, every date, he'd come to know more and more that he was wishing she had never got herself mixed up with Ian. And not just for his sister's sake.

It was for his own.

I want her for myself—with no other complications, no strategy or plots or machinations or ulterior motives.

Heaviness filled him. It didn't matter what he wanted for himself, he thought savagely. What he did he did for Eva. That was what he had to remember. That was all he had to remember.

And time was running out. He would have only a brief window while Ian and Eva were away together in the USA to achieve his aim of seducing Marisa Milburne and taking her away from his brother-in-law.

Which was why he was now, two days after the Sunday roast in her apartment, sitting here in a restaurant off Holland Park Avenue, waiting for her to open the white envelope he'd proffered.

Marisa was still gazing down at it. She'd accepted the dinner invitation only with reluctance. She had to stop this. She really did. She was getting in too deep.

She had managed the previous day, right after her dangerous dinner *à deux* with Athan Teodarkis in her apartment, finally to meet up with Ian for lunch. His face had told her what she'd dreaded hearing.

'I have to go to San Francisco. I can't get out of it. There's no one else that can handle it, and I've had my marching orders from the top.'

Her face had fallen. 'How long for, do you think?'

'I'm not sure—at least a week, probably more,' he'd said apologetically. 'The thing is…' He took a breath, looked even more apologetic. 'Eva's got the idea of turning it into a holiday—flying on from SF to Hawaii. So I could easily be away three weeks or more.'

Even as he'd said 'Hawaii' she'd felt a pang of envy dart through her.

Hawaii…tropical beaches…palm trees…silver sand…

But it would not be *her* there. She was stuck in London—where the weather had turned vicious. The bright but cold sunshine that had filled the Holland Park Orangery had given way to a miserable, dull and biting cold, with a low cloud base and an icy wind. Spring seemed a long way off. Even just getting out of the cab when she and Athan had arrived at the restaurant had set the wind whipping around her stockinged legs. Now she sat with her legs slanted against the radiator against which their table was situated.

'Well?' prompted Athan, indicating the envelope. There was an expression in his eyes she could not read.

It looked, she thought curiously, like anticipation.

She turned her attention back to the envelope he so wanted her to open. Carefully she slit it with a table knife and shook out the contents. As she did so, her eyes widened.

'You said you wanted a tropical beach,' she heard him murmur.

But she was gazing, rapt, at the leaflet that was lying there. A palm tree, an azure sea, a silvered beach, and in the background a low-rise, thatch-roofed resort, fronted by a vast swimming pool even more azure than the lapping sea.

Projecting from the leaflet were two airline tickets.

'Come with me,' said Athan.

His voice was soft. Intimate. Persuasive.

Marisa lifted her head to look at him—and drowned.

Drowned in what she saw in his eyes, unmasked, unveiled…

Her lips parted, the breath stilling in her throat.

Her hand was taken, folded into his. It was the first time he'd touched her so deliberately—only in that first, formal raising of her hand to his lips, that faint, brief grazing of his fingertips against her cheek, had he ever made contact with her. But this—this warm, strong hand-clasp—seemed to envelop her whole being, not just her hand lying there inert, helpless in his grasp.

'Come with me,' he said again. 'Be with me.'

Emotion rushed through her like heady wine in her veins. Like a cloud of butterflies suddenly taking flight inside her. His clasp strengthened and his thumb stroked along the edge of her palm. Intimately. Possessively.

His eyes poured into hers. So dark, so deep, flecked with gold that glinted in the candlelight, that drowned her, sweeping her away.

His thumb indented into the soft flesh of her palm. She could feel its pressure, feel the power of his touch—its persuasion.

'Say yes—it's all I ask.'

Hadn't she always known this must happen? Hadn't she felt it from the moment she'd set eyes on him? Hadn't her heart skipped and her blood pulsed, her breath caught? Hadn't she known every time she'd been with him that this was what she wanted—dreamt of—desired?

He saw her yielding. Saw her features soften, her eyes fill with a lambent lustre that told him everything he wanted to know. Triumph filled him. He had got her—finally. She would not refuse him now. She would not continue to hold him at bay, to treat him as if he were forbidden fruit. Now she would yield to him—taste the fruit he offered her.

And he—oh, he would do likewise. He would take this time with her and make her his own. Put aside, even if only for a brief few weeks, all his worries about his sister and her troubled marriage, put aside all his fears for her, his doubts about her fickle husband.

For now—just for now—he would do what every moment with Marisa had confirmed to him. That what he wanted was her—all to himself.

Away from everything that cast a damning shadow over her.

Just the two of them—together.

Only that.

CHAPTER THREE

'WHAT do you think? Worth the long-haul flight?'

The familiar note of amusement was in Athan's voice as he posed his question. He knew what the answer would be. Had known it from the moment they'd landed, stepped out into the balmy, tropical heat seven thousand miles south west from bleak, icy London. Knew it now, as they stood side by side on the little wooden veranda of their beachside cabana.

Marisa turned to gaze at him. 'How can you ask?' she breathed. Then she turned back again. Back to look at the scene in front of her.

It was exactly like the photo in the brochure—but real. And she was *here*—here in the middle of it all! Like a dream—a wonderful, exotic dream.

And the Caribbean beach—silver sanded, backed with palms swaying in the gentle calypso breeze that rustled the scarlet hibiscus and the fragrant frangipani blooms—was not the only dream come true.

So was the man at her side.

She could feel her breath catch as it had caught over and over again during their journey here, cocooned in first class seats. Her eyes had been wide with the excitement not just of travelling abroad for the first time, or because it was first class, with all the pandering and luxury that came with it, but most of all because of the man sitting beside her.

She had made the right decision in accepting his invitation to come here. She knew it—felt it. For how could it be otherwise? How could she possibly have resisted what he'd offered her? The question was rhetorical; her answer was a given. It was impossible to resist Athan Teodarkis! Impossible to resist his invitation—both to this wonderful holiday with him and, she thought, with a shiver of quivering awareness, to what else he was inviting.

There had been, it was true, a momentary pang when she'd thought of Ian—but it had been swiftly quenched. Ian was far away—and if her alternative was to stay languishing in London, without him, what was to hold her there when she might be here…on this palm-fringed tropical beach?

With Athan.

Day after day, every time she met with him, her response to him intensified. She became more and more vividly aware of the effect he could have on her. It might be foolish, it might be rash—but it was so powerful this rush that came whenever she thought of him, whenever she was with him.

I can't resist him—can't resist what he's offering me. I can't…

And for this brief idyllic time, here in this tropical paradise he'd brought her to, she would resist nothing of what he offered her.

She gave a little sigh of pleasure at the view ahead of her—the time with Athan ahead of her. Happiness filled her, and a wonderful sense of carefreeness. Whatever else was complicated or difficult or troubling in her life this time was not going to be part of. This time was for her—and for the man she was with so willingly.

'I'm glad not to disappoint,' he said.

For a long, bewitching moment his eyes caressed her. Then, as if reluctantly, his expression changed.

'What would you like to do first?' he asked.

She had no hesitation as she answered, 'I can't resist that sea! It's calling out to me!'

He gave a laugh. 'And to me. OK—let's hit the beach, then.'

He ushered her indoors and she stepped through into the shady interior of the cabana. It was designed as if it were a simple, palm-roofed hut, but it was a simplicity that belied a level of luxury that went with the whole ambience of the resort.

On the flight over Athan had regaled her about the island and what awaited them there.

'St Cecile has been fortunate to escape mass tourism,' he'd told her. 'It's a little too off the beaten track, so until recently it's been something of a backwater. But to my mind that's all to the good. In the last ten years or so there has been some very careful development for tourism, but at the most upmarket end, so the handful of resorts are well separated from each other, and beautifully sited and landscaped. It's a little gem of an island, to my mind.'

Even without anything to compare it with, having seen it, Marisa could only wholeheartedly agree. It was like stepping into one of those luxury travel magazines, she thought. A place most people could never visit.

And I am! she thought, with another little rush of excitement.

With a companion anyone would swoon over…

She slipped into the bedroom. As they had followed the bellhop from the main resort building along sandy, shell-lined paths amongst the palm trees and entered their cabana she had felt a little flutter of nerves on seeing the one bedroom. Somehow it had made very real just what this holiday would entail.

So was it nerves she had felt, or a flutter of excitement? Anticipation?

She felt it again now, as she searched through her suitcase for her bikini. She had bought it in a mad hectic rush spent raiding the West End stores the day before flying out, and now, as she looked at it lying on the counterpane, she felt another flurry of nerves. In the changing room she had felt brave about it—its brevity had seemed entirely right for such an exotic destination. But now, realising that she was about to don it and emerge in it, displaying herself to a man who up till now had only seen her in high-coverage winter clothes, it was unnerving to say the least.

Nevertheless, she had bought it to be worn and to be seen in it. Even so, before she emerged on to the veranda she draped a matching voile sarong around her, which gave her a layer of veiling she was thankful for when, some moments later, Athan emerged as well.

His eyes went to her immediately, visibly drinking her in. For all the fine voile veiling her, she still felt acutely revealed. But if Athan were drinking *her* in, she had to acknowledge she was doing exactly the same to him. He was wearing a pair of hip-hugging dark blue boardies, and his torso was completely exposed. Marisa felt her eyes widen automatically.

Bare-chested, Athan was everything she'd imagined him to be—and more. Lean packed, with not an ounce of spare flesh on him, yet not overtly muscular. His smooth, tanned skin moulded over taut muscle, planed down over perfect pecs and delineated abs to arrow towards the low-slung waistband of his board shorts.

She dragged her gaze away.

'Race you to the sea!' she exclaimed, with slightly forced gaiety.

She turned to descend the wide shallow steps that led down to a path to the sea, a dozen metres or so beyond, set between palm trees framing the vista. But a hand stayed her, catching her shoulder.

'Wait—have you got sunblock on?'

She twisted her head back. 'Yes—loads.'

He nodded. 'Good. It's essential in this latitude. My skin

can take more exposure than yours, being naturally darker, but even so I have to use it copiously. You—' his eyes washed over her '—with your English rose complexion, must be totally protected. It would be sacrilege,' he told her, his voice changing suddenly so that it seemed to caress her as much as his eyes, 'to burn such pale, tender skin.'

As he spoke his touch at her shoulder softened, echoing the caress of his eyes and voice. She felt her pulse skip a beat, butterflies flutter in her stomach.

'OK, let's race!' He dropped his hand and surged forward, vaulting down the steps to the sandy pathway.

'Cheat!' she called out indignantly, and unfastening her wrap started after him.

Inevitably he reached the sea first and plunged in, diving headfirst into the aqua water as soon as he was barely waist-deep. Moments later she followed suit, feeling the water close like liquid silk over her. She surfaced, hair streaming down her bare back, water droplets glistening like diamonds all over her body.

Athan could only stare. It was impossible not to. *Thee mou*, but she was glorious. Like a sea nymph, a nereid foam-born as the translucent water washed around her—and as divinely beautiful as such a creature of ancient myth.

He had known right from the first that she was beautiful, and had seen with his own eyes that her figure was perfect, but to see it all now, so gloriously displayed in only the skimpiest of coverings, veiled only by the water itself, was breath stopping.

But even as he stood and gazed he could feel conflict writhing within him. How beautiful she was—how he desired her…. He wanted only to catch her in a rush of diamond water and feel her body close to his. Yet, like a flicker across his synapses, seeking to block the vivid visual image before him, came a whisper of warning.

Take care. She is beautiful, yes, and you desire her—how

could you not? But do not forget—do not allow yourself to forget—just why you are here. For what purpose...

Impatiently, he pushed the warning aside. There would be time for that later, when they returned to England, but for now he could set aside all that and focus only on the glorious fact that he was here with Marisa.

A sense of well-being descended on him as if from the hot, bright sun overhead. This was good—more than good. He was here, in this beautiful place, and the rest of the world with all its cares and worries, was an ocean away. This beautiful, breath-catching woman was for him—for him alone! Anticipation creamed through him.

'This is heavenly!' Marisa's voice was full. She lay back, giving herself to the water, letting the buoyancy of the sea support her as she bobbed gently in the gentle swell.

The sun poured down its blessing on her, and she had to close her eyes fully against its strength. Her arms drifted out as she rested on the bosom of the sea. How long she floated she wasn't sure, because time was drifting now, just as her body was. Until she felt two hands lightly on her shoulders, slowly starting to turn her like a starfish.

'I don't like to wake you, but I think, for the first time in this climate, you should probably come out now,' Athan told her. 'Your body feels cool, but the sun's rays still do their work, and more, even reflected off the sea.'

Reluctantly she let her feet sink down to the soft sand and stood up. Sunlight was glancing off Athan's tanned body, turning him to bronze, a sculpted work of art. She could not tear her eyes away, and he gave her his slanting smile.

'It's the same for me,' he said, his voice low, his meaning clear.

She felt her cheeks flush and dipped under the water again, making a show of smoothing out her hair as she re-emerged.

She waded towards the shore and as she gained the beach could feel the sun baking down on her back.

'Time for a shower,' Athan said, and immediately Marisa wished he hadn't. It conjured images that she had to banish straight away.

'Me first,' she said laughingly, and ran up the steps of the cabana, gaining the tiled bathroom before him.

The water sluicing down on her was not tepid and brackish, but beautifully refreshing, and she quickly gave her hair a light shampoo with the courtesy bottle provided. Feeling naked, she wrapped herself in one of the generous soft fleecy towels and emerged, wringing out her hair, and then her skimpy bikini, and wandered out on to their veranda to drape the wet bikini over the rail. It would dry fast, she knew, even in the shade.

The sun was lowering in the sky. Facing westwards, towards the sheltered Caribbean shore, the beach would be a fabulous place to watch it set, she realised. A little to the left of their cabana was a structure like a fixed palanquin, with a huge bleached canvas mattress and a matching awning. Generous cushions tumbled on the surface, and the edges turned into a kind of tabletop—to put drinks on, she reckoned.

Combing out her hair, she gazed out at the peaceful scene. She could tell there were other cabanas along the shoreline, but such was the distribution of vegetation and palms that each seemed to have its own portion of beach. It was designed, she realised, to be totally private.

Intimate.

Another of those electric flutterings skittered across her nerve endings. How would the evening end? she wondered.

But she knew—of course she knew! There could be only one way to end such an evening. Only one outcome beneath the tropical stars.

She would be in Athan's arms... She felt her heart give a little skip, her lungs a little squeeze.

How wonderful life was! To grant her this—so idyllic a place—and such a man as Athan to experience it with.

To experience far more than this beautiful island...

With a delicious shiver of anticipation she headed indoors to get dressed. It was too early yet to change for dinner, so instead she put on one of the lovely loose fine cotton sundresses she'd bought, with narrow straps and almost ankle length. Not bothering to put on a bra—it was too hot for that!—she slipped her feet into a pair of flip-flops, shook out her hair the better to dry it, and wandered into the little lounge-diner that the front of the cabana opened into.

She could hear the shower running, indicating that Athan had taken her place there, and she wandered across to the fridge set into the mahogany sideboard. She took out a carton of mango and orange juice, diluting it with chilled water before heading outdoors again. The shaded palanquin looked so inviting that she drifted in its direction, settling herself back with a comfortable sigh against the piled-up cushions.

'So this is where you are.' A deep voice sounded lazily behind her.

Marisa half crooked her neck and saw Athan approaching. He had changed into a pair of long cotton shorts and a pale blue short sleeved shirt, open at the neck. He looked cool, casual, and completely devastating.

He, too, had a glass in his hand.

'It's a little too early for a sundowner, but the moment that sun hits the deck I'm going to crack open the bottle of champagne that's in the fridge,' he told her with a grin. 'Till then, it's fruit juice only.'

'Me too,' she answered with a smile.

He climbed lightly up onto the mattress, but lounged back at the far end. Marisa was grateful. It was so overwhelming, this whole experience of being here with Athan, knowing what was to come, wanting to savour ever step of the journey.

I don't want to rush things, she thought. *I want them to be perfect.*

Unforgettable!

So for now it was perfect just to sit there, comfortably in her own space, with Athan unpressurised company, relaxed and carefree.

'I can't really believe I'm here,' she mused. 'It is just *so* unbearably gorgeous. Like being in a dream.'

'Oh, it's real all right.' Athan's voice was dryly amused.

But there was something else in it—some note she couldn't identify. She glanced at him.

He was looking at her, but just as in his voice there was something in his eyes she could not see—as if he were holding something back from her. Then, a moment later, it was gone as he leant forward to clink glasses with her.

'To a holiday we'll never forget,' he said. His eyes were warm, caressing.

'I'll never forget this!' she breathed.

For the briefest second that strange, half-hidden look was back in his eyes.

'No, you won't,' he agreed.

Then it was gone, and he was taking a long draft from his glass, turning his head to look out over the sea, where the sun was lowering its golden orb towards the waiting embrace of the ocean.

*Just like I am waiting for Athan's embrace...*thought Marisa dreamily.

They sat half in silence, half in companionable chit-chat, listening to the warm wind soughing in the tops of the palms, the gentle susurration of the wavelets breaking on the silver shore. It was so incredibly quiet and peaceful they might have been the only people on the beach or even the island, Marisa thought.

'Is that actually a coconut?' she asked, her gaze drifting to the top of one of the nearby palms.

Athan gave a laugh. 'Do you think it's a fake one, then?' he challenged, amused.

'Maybe the hotel ties fake ones to the tops of the palm trees to impress the visitors,' she responded, entering into the spirit of the banter.

'We'll ask one of the garden staff to get it down for us, if you like,' Athan said. 'You should see them climb palm trees. It's quite ingenious—they use a short length of rope which they hook around the trunk, then use it to lever themselves up to the top—it's quite a skill!'

'You sound like you've seen it before,' she said.

'Well, not here,' he admitted. 'I've never been to this resort before.'

That, of course, was why he'd chosen it. He wasn't known here, and he was unlikely to bump into anyone who knew him. Or his sister. Besides, this resort was specifically aimed at couples who wanted to get totally away from it all—including any other couples.

That was what made it so ideal a place for him to bring Marisa Milburne.

Remote, luxurious, discreet. Perfect for his intentions.

A shadow of a flicker fleeted across his face. She was so trusting of him—lounging there, sipping her juice, gazing out over the vista ahead, her pose relaxed and graceful.

Should I really do this?

The question he didn't want to hear came from nowhere—sliding like a needle under his consciousness.

His conscience?

You've brought her here to make her want you instead of him.

And she did want him! Wanted him as much as he wanted her—all his senses told him so. And for that reason he crushed down his disquiet.

England, his sister, his philandering brother-in-law—all seemed very, very far away.

And Marisa…ah, she was blissfully close.

He raised his glass to her again. 'To us,' he said softly.

And her eyes glowed like jewels in the golden light of the setting sun.

Marisa narrowed her eyes in concentration, listening intently. One of the serving staff was talking to another islander, and she was trying to make out what they were saying.

She abandoned the attempt, turning her attention back to Athan, sitting opposite her at the table.

'Do you know, I can't make out a single word?' she said. 'It doesn't even sound like English.'

'It isn't,' he told her, amused. 'The island Creole is French-based, dating from the time when St Cecile was ruled by France, but it also includes fragments of African languages, as well as the original Carib languages. Don't worry if you can't understand it—outsiders seldom do. All the island Creoles across the Caribbean have virtually evolved into their own languages. They have their own literature as well, and these days there's a real effort to preserve them for future generations of islanders.'

Marisa shook her head. 'It doesn't sound like French, either,' she admitted.

She glanced across at Athan. He was looking, as the habitual little catch in her throat informed her, lethally attractive. Since lolling on the palanquin—where they had, as he had promised, toasted each other in champagne as the sun set—he'd changed into tan chinos and another short-sleeved open-necked shirt, and he looked disgustingly, casually gorgeous. His sable hair was slightly feathered, and his relaxed pose seemed to emphasise the lean, muscled power of his body.

What she wanted to do, she knew, was simply sit there and gaze at him. But what she had to do, she also knew, was keep chatting to him to stop herself being reduced to such a gormless level. It was hard, though—and not just because of her own sharpened awareness of him. It was also because he had the devastating habit of relaxing back in his chair and letting his gaze wash over her, making no bones about showing that he liked what he was seeing.

That he liked it very much...

Again that flutter in her stomach came, and she knew that the effort she'd made to look her absolute best tonight was paying off. After the champagne on the beach she'd disappeared into the bathroom, taking excruciating care over her make-up—not too much for the climate and setting, but enough to enhance her eyes to the maximum—glossing her lips with dew, and styling her hair so that it looked artlessly tumbled. Her choice of clothes was equally careful. A long dress in a swirling mix of vermilions and gold, with spaghetti straps and a high waist that made her seem taller and more slender. She'd wrapped a piece of filmy gauze picked out in the same vermilion and gold thread around her shoulders. The temperature had dropped, but by very little—the night was sweet and balmy, as caressing as a silken touch to her skin.

Now, as she lifted her wine glass to her lips, the golden sheen from her narrow gilt bangles catching the candlelight, she knew that she had got the look just right. Other couples were dining in the main restaurant as well, though each table was afforded privacy by potted palms and brilliant bougainvillaea, and the whole dining area formed almost a semicircle around the resort pool which glowed, unearthly, with underwater lights.

All my life, she thought hazily, I'll remember this. This wonderful, magical place, this wonderful, magical evening.

This wonderful, magical man who had made it all come true for her...

But she couldn't just go on staring helplessly at him.

'So, when did the island become English, then?' she asked, infusing interest into her voice.

'I believe it swapped hands several times—depending on the fortunes of war and various treaties between France and England during the eighteenth century. But it ended up being definitely English after the Napoleonic Wars. One of the perks of victory,' Athan said dryly. 'The French owners of the plantations kept their property, however, so they didn't mind too much. As for the slaves—well, I guess they benefited in the end by being emancipated in 1834, which was earlier than in the remaining French colonies.'

A troubled expression lit Marisa's eyes. 'It casts a long shadow, doesn't it, slavery? Over such a beautiful place?'

Athan reached for his wine glass, taking a reflective mouthful. 'It's long been one of the ironies of Greek civilisation,' he observed, 'that whilst the modern world pays tribute to ancient Greek democracy their economy relied entirely on slave labour.'

She frowned. 'It seems dreadful that slavery was able to flourish again after Europeans discovered the Americas. It was so obviously an evil thing.'

'Oh, it's easy enough to persuade yourself that your behaviour is justified when it benefits you materially,' Athan replied.

His eyes rested on her, and he saw a momentarily discomfited expression in her face. Was she thinking about how she herself was perfectly happy to let Ian Randall house and keep her?

Yet even as he speculated he felt his own thoughts prick at him.

And you—what about you? You say you are doing all this to help save your sister's marriage—yet you are benefiting from it yourself, aren't you? Having this beautiful, desirable woman for yourself!

But he didn't want to think about being back in England.

Didn't want to think about what he would have to say to
Marisa then, and why. Didn't want to think about his sister, let alone his pernicious brother-in-law. Didn't want to
do anything at all, except savour this moment to the full—
enjoy the time he had here, the days and nights he would
have with Marisa.

All to himself, without the outside world to trouble him
with its disquieting, uncomfortable imperatives.

And that was just what he would do! Enjoy this time, rel-
ish it and experience it to the full.

He set down his glass, resumed his meal. It was exquisitely
cooked—a concoction of grilled fish, caught that day, fla-
voured with sweet spices. Marisa was eating breaded prawns,
each on a separate skewer, with a rich coconut dipping sauce.

She'd picked up another skewer a moment or two after
he'd made his pointed observation, and now busied herself
swirling it into the sauce.

'Are they good?' he enquired. The amused, lazy note was
back in his voice. The mordant expression in his face gone
completely. He would keep it that way. Why spoil what this
evening would bring? What each golden day here would
bring? Each velvet night...

'Fabulous!' she said. 'Though I think each one's about a
million calories.'

'You can atone by only having fruit for dessert,' he said
smilingly.

She glanced at him again as she took a delicate mouthful of the sauce-swathed prawn. That sudden austerity in his
face had gone, and she was relieved. She wondered what had
caused it. But it was gone now, and that was good enough
for her peace of mind. She didn't want anything to spoil this
idyll...

Atoning for her rich main course by eating fruit for dessert
certainly didn't spoil things—the slices of luscious tropical
fruit, served on crushed ice, were as delicious as the most cal-

orific pudding. Athan dipped in and out of the heaped mound sporadically, lounging back in his chair, swirling a glass of brandy in his fingers. For herself, she wanted no more alcohol. The earlier champagne, together with wine over dinner, had made the world a sweet, hazy place.

A sense of absolute well-being filled her. Absolute happiness…That was the thought coiling in and out of her synapses. Because how could she be happier than to be here, in this warm, balmy paradise, with a man like Athan Teodarkis? Who was looking at her now with such an expression in his incredibly gorgeous eyes…

She gave a little inward shiver of excitement—anticipation, feelings that only mounted as, coffee consumed, Athan got to his feet.

'Shall we?' he said, and held his hand out to her.

She took it, and he drew her up, not relinquishing her hand. They strolled around the pool, and it seemed, Marisa thought, so absolutely right to be doing so hand in hand. He made casual conversation and she answered in kind, keeping the note easy and relaxed, even though inside her she could feel her blood pulsing.

Beyond the pool the landscaped gardens gave way to more sandy ground, with low green vegetation, and the tiled paved area dispersed into multiple little pathways, each one marked by shelled edges and lit at strategic intervals by lights set either low at the base of palm trees or hung high on ornamental stands. As they neared their cabana she could hear the gentle shooshing of the sea, the endless chitter of the cicadas in the bushes, and the insistent chirruping of the tree frogs.

They strolled down on to the beach that fronted their cabana. A moon was hanging low over the sea, and there was a sheen of moonlight on the water. A mild breeze teased, but the night was warm. She could feel the humidity in it like an embracing net around her.

She gazed upwards. Stars as brilliant as golden lamps

blazed in the heavens. She felt dizzy just gazing upwards—dizzy on champagne, on the sweet tropical air, on the blood pulsing in her veins. She seemed to sway...

Hands came around her waist, steadying her. Her gaze dropped down to mingle with his. Even in the moonlight she could see his expression. What he was telling her. She felt his hands at her waist, light and warm, fingers splayed. The pulse in her blood strengthened.

He murmured her name, and then came what she had been waiting for, yearning for all evening. From the moment she'd first seen him and felt her heart flutter at the sight of him, at the impact he made on her. Slowly, exquisitely, agonisingly slowly, his mouth descended.

His kiss was light, like a feather, teasing at her lips, playing with them, playing with her desire for him, with his for her. Only when it seemed to her she could bear it no longer did she feel the sudden impress of his splayed fingertips and the simultaneous deepening of his kiss—as if he, too, had been unable to resist longer.

Sensation made her swoon, and she could feel her heart turning over and over as his mouth took hers richly, deeply, with a warm, insistent passion that dominated every sense in her body. There was only this moment, only this kiss, in all the world...

It lasted an eternity—it lasted only the briefest moment of time. He drew back from her, his gaze pouring into hers. She felt liquid, boneless.

'I want you so much...' His voice was a low husk.

She could only sway in his clasp, lifting her mouth to his again, aching and yearning for his touch.

'I am yours,' she whispered.

Triumph glistened in his eyes and he gave a low rasp in his throat as he kissed her again, hungrily, voraciously, sweeping her up into his arms and carrying her off the beach, up on to the veranda and into their cabana.

The air was warm inside, for they had not put the air-con-
ditioning on, and in the bedroom, as he lowered her to the
turned-down bed, the heat was a cocoon around them.

Her body seemed aflame—all her senses aflame. Swiftly,
skilfully, he slid her dress from her body, baring her to his
view in the dim light. She slipped her arms up above her head,
so that her breasts lifted. His eyes were hungry for them,
his lips hungrier. She could hear him murmur something in
Greek, but her whole being was focussed only on the sensations he was arousing.

Dear God, but it was blissful—blissful! Like softest velvet, finest silk, laving and teasing and arousing her, until her
body was flickering with unseen fire, her head twisting, her
stomach taut. Then his mouth closed over the crested coral
peaks, suckling and caressing with his lips, his tongue. A
sound came from her throat—primitive, powerful. His mouth
slipped from her breasts, easing down over the smooth, taut
line of her abdomen. His hands shaped her slender waist,
splaying upwards so that the tips of his fingers could continue to tease her straining nipples, squeezing and nipping
them so that eddy after eddy of sensation shimmered through
her, each setting up a wave that was growing in power as he
drew from her the response he sought.

Restless hunger started to fill her. She wanted more—so
much more! She wanted *him*. Her hands reached for him,
clutching over his shoulders, tugging his shirt from him in
movements that became increasingly hurried and impatient.
He paused in his ministrations, shrugging the garment from
him, and while he was at it shedding the rest of his clothes as
well. With a gasp, she realised that he was completely naked
now—completely hers!

With a little moan she drew him down on her, feeling the
warm, hard length of his body—feeling, too, with a thrill,
the full power of his masculinity. Her reaction was instinctive. Her hips lifted to his as he responded, one iron hard

thigh slipping between hers. His mouth was on hers now, and her hands were running along the sculpted lines of his back, eagerly tracing its moulded contours. His skin was like cool satin, and she gloried in the sensations she was clearly able to arouse in him as she trailed her fingertips delicately along his spine.

Urgency filled him. Desire was peaking in him and he wanted...needed...to fulfil it. She was afire for him, and he for her. The sweet softness of her body, yielding to his, was all he craved. He sought her, shifting his weight until he found what he desired. He arched over her, his hands shaping her shoulders as her hips arched questingly to his. For one long, endless moment he gazed down into her face, transfixed by what he was arousing in her.

Theos, but she was so, so beautiful! Her hair streaming across the pillows. Her face alight with an unearthly beauty. Her slender body aroused and yearning for his. It was a yearning that he matched, met...surpassed in every aching part of him.

Now, *now* he needed fulfilment—needed to be fused with her, melded to her core, to become one with her.

He heard her murmur his name, sounding urgent, so urgent in her need for him. Felt her hands press at his back to close him to her, to fuse herself against him.

With a surge he was there, filling her deeply, fully, feeling her close around him, hearing her cry out, hearing his own voice soothing her even as every synapse in his brain started an insistent, driving firing that swept across his consciousness.

His body started to move in an age-old, primeval rhythm, possessing him even as he now possessed her. She was threshing against him and it drove him wild, crazy for her, for what she was doing to him, for the way her incredible body was lifting to his, fusing to his, with a hunger, an insistence that he was answering. He was taking her with him on his urgent,

storming journey to more and ever more peaks of sensation
that heated every portion of his flesh to a white heat.

Her eyes were fluttering, their pupils so distended they
seemed to flood her eyes even as sensation flooded her
body—sensation such as she had never felt before. A storm
of quickening that was sweeping her higher, always higher,
higher—

Time stopped—it had no meaning. There was only this
moment, this endless, incredible *now* of sensation, rippling
through her body, melting her, fusing her. Her hands clung
to him, her throat arched back, her hips pressed against his
to take him within her, catching at him again and yet again.
And with each stroke he was taking her further and higher
and deeper. And the pleasure, the bliss, was so intense, so
incredible, so absolute that when the storm broke within her
she seemed to be consumed by it, as the storm drove through
her, buckling and convulsing her.

She cried out. She could hear it. And it was a cry that went
on and on, just as the storm within her went on and on, and it
was another world, another existence, another *her*...one she
had never known, never dreamt existed.

Then another voice joined hers—deep-throated, hoarse,
as urgent as hers, as insistent. She felt his body fill her, felt
the culmination of that endless driving rhythm, felt him soar-
ing with her into that other world that was consuming her,
so that her whole body had become a living, burning flame.

For long moments she was bathed in the fire, as if its flickering heat enveloped them both, making them one, making them unified, melded together. Then, when their sated,
exhausted bodies could take no more, she felt the burning
begin to ebb, the throbbing of her core lessen, die slowly to
stillness. Ease. Leaving in its wake not ashes, but a sweetness—a sense of wellbeing so absolute that it bathed her in
a profound wonder.

She could only let her fingers drift across his back, feeling the exhaustion of every limb as they lay wound about each other and the last lingering flickers of the consuming flames died gently away.

How long she lay there, entwined with him, she did not know. Knew only that she had found a place to be that she never wanted to leave. Here in Athan's arms, in his enveloping embrace, was world enough for her. Drifting in and out of sleep, she lay holding him close against her breast.

Close against her heart…

Marisa swam lazily towards the pool's swim-up bar. As she neared it the pool shallowed, and she waded the rest of the way before perching herself on one of the little half submerged stone stools. The barman sauntered along to her from his side, and asked in the lilting island accent what she would like. Opting for a virgin strawberry margarita, Marisa sat sipping through the crushed scarlet-coloured ice and gazed peacefully out over the turquoise water of the pool and the azure sea beyond.

Even after nearly two weeks here she still could not get enough of the vista before her. She gave a little sigh of happiness. Just as she could not get enough of Athan.

Not that she had to do without him. She was with him just about twenty-four-seven. There was only a brief daily interval when, as he was doing now, he checked into the resort business centre and communicated, as briefly as he could get away with, his direct reports, and received any unavoidable updates. But he was seldom gone for more than half an hour. Other than that they were together all the time.

A ripple of wonder went through her. She had known from the moment she'd yielded to his invitation to come here with him that this time with him would be unforgettable, but never had she realised just how much so.

And it wasn't just the sex—although even saying 'just the sex' was a universe away from describing the incredible, transforming experience it was every time. No, it wasn't 'just sex' at all. How could it be when it seemed to her that her very being caught fire, was consumed like a phoenix, to be reborn in that moment of ecstasy, enveloped in his arms? Surely it wasn't 'just sex' to be so consumed by passion for him—to want him and crave him not only in the fires of consummation but in the peaceful, languorous aftermath that wrapped them in its sweet, honeyed balm, when they simply lay together, softly caressing each other, all passion spent, their eyes entwining with each other, drowsy with satiation. To sleep in his arms, cradled by him, holding him close to her, only to wake later, in the long reaches of the tropical night, when he would start to make love to her again, as if he could not get enough of her.

Yet even as her eyes softened with the memory of his ardent, transforming lovemaking a haunted look fleeted therein. This idyll here on St Cecile was nearly over. Soon, in a day or two, they would be headed for home—back to London. Back to their normal lives.

What would happen then?

Disquiet plucked at her, disturbing her contentment. What would happen when they were back in England, away from here?

Could the idyll continue?

That was the question that coiled and uncoiled inside her head. She had shut it out, not let herself think about it, but over the last few days, as their second week had started to ebb away, day by precious day, she had felt it plucking at her consciousness, wanting to be answered.

But she didn't want to answer it. Didn't want to think what the answer might be—what she feared it would be.

This *was* an idyll—a blissful, unforgettable *intermezzo*—in a tropical paradise where reality seemed as distant as the British winter. But what would happen when the *intermezzo* was over?

Oh, Athan was as passionate, as ardent as any woman could want—could dream of—but that was here. What would happen back in London?

Doubts fed her disquiet. Yes, Athan was hers *here,* but even here, these last days, she had felt him withdraw from her sometimes—only briefly, but distinctly. It was not a physical withdrawal but much more disquieting than that. It was a kind of mental withdrawal, as though their casual intimacy was draining away. Sometimes there was a look in his eye, she was sure of it, when he seemed to be looking at her with a stranger's gaze. Then, a moment later, it would be gone and he would be his normal self again—and she would wonder if she had merely imagined it.

She could reason so well, she knew. He was a man of affairs who had a business empire to run—how could he possibly be confined only to focussing on her? She had to accept that his mind would go from time to time to matters of greater import.

Greater import than herself.

An ache started within her. A flickering of fear. A fear she didn't want to face.

Fear of a time she did not want to face.

But it would come, for all that. The hours were ticking inexorably towards that time. The sun's passage in the sky was arcing towards that time. It would come, fear it as she might—dread it as she did.

He says words of passion to me—but only passion. He smiles at me, and holds my hand, and walks at my side, and takes me in his arms—but what does he feel for me? Is it only passion? Only desire?

She could not answer—dared not answer. And dared not answer an even more fearful question.

What do I feel for him? Only passion? Only desire?

Yes! It had to be. It had to be only that and nothing more. She must allow it to be nothing else. Because when this idyll here was over, when the island was only a faint invisible sliver of land half a world away, and their reality was once more the busy wintry streets of London, then she would discover a truth she dared not know yet—a truth she feared.

What if he is done with me?

She took a heavy breath, staring sightlessly out over the blindingly bright water.

I have to prepare for that. I have to prepare for when he turns to me and tells me what I fear to hear.

That he was done with her.

No! She would not think ahead to that moment. She would not spoil these last precious days with Athan by dwelling on what might come. She would not cast the shadow of such fear over what she had now.

Resolute, she finished her fruit juice and got out of the pool. Athan would have finished at the business centre soon and be heading back to the cabana. Marisa wanted to be there waiting for him. As hungry for him as he always was for her. Mid-morning passion was so very, very enjoyable…

Putting her dark thoughts firmly aside, she set off, her steps eager.

Athan smoothed the silken hair, holding Marisa's slender body against his. They were both drowsy in the aftermath of lovemaking. The low swirl of the overhead fan was the only noise. Soon they would rouse themselves and shower, and then dress for lunch. Not that lunch was in the slightest bit formal. Everyone wore beach clothes, possibly with the lightest cover-up and nothing more.

Lunch was a leisurely, relaxed affair, mostly salads and fruits, served from a huge buffet in the open air dining room shaded by wide awnings from the heat of the noonday sun. The constant gentle breeze gave a welcome cooling, and the lap of the pool water added to the lazy, easy atmosphere.

But then the whole resort exuded a lazy, easy atmosphere. Relaxation was inevitable.

Except that right now Athan was not feeling relaxed in the slightest. It was not because of their recent passionate consummation—it had another cause. An unwelcome one.

There were only two more days left of the holiday, and then they would be flying back to London.

He could feel his muscles tense momentarily. And in London he would have to confront Marisa—tell her just why he had taken her on holiday here, and what that reason meant for her. And for his brother-in-law. It would mean the impossibility of any relationship between her and Ian.

But even as he reminded himself of the reason he'd brought her here he could feel his mind rebelling. Maybe there was no need to spell it out to her. After all, surely if she'd just spent two weeks with another man she couldn't possibly think of going back to Ian? Surely she would take it for granted that her time with Ian was over, and that was that.

So maybe I don't have to confront her.

One thing was for sure: he didn't want to. Right from the start he'd known it wasn't going to be easy—that it was going to be unpleasant and uncomfortable. But now, after all that they had here, together, it was going to be a whole lot more than just 'unpleasant'....

I can't do it.

Revulsion filled him. How could he? How could he go from holding her in his arms to denouncing her as a marriage breaker? How could he make love to her and then accuse her?

He'd known, of course—he'd known all along—that that was what he was going to have to do, but it was one thing to plan cold-bloodedly to seduce the woman who was threatening his sister's marriage and quite another, he thought hollowly, to spend two weeks with her and then have to face the ugly denouement that he'd envisaged delivering.

I must have been mad to think of such a scheme!

Mad to think that he could carry it out.

Madness to think that I could hold her in my arms like this and still be planning such a denunciation of her.

His eyes stared up at the rotating fan. Its movement echoed his thoughts, going round and endlessly round in his head. He knew what he had set out to do—what was coming closer and closer with every passing hour—knew that the very thought of it was building to a mountain of impossibility inside him.

An impossibility because of Marisa herself.

Even as he said her name silently in his head he could feel his response to it. Felt his arm tighten around her waist as she slept against him. Felt the rightness of her being there, in his arms...

I didn't know it was going to be like this. I knew I wanted her, desired her—but I never dreamt that the possession would be so...incredible!

Everything had seemed to come together. The passion flaring between them, their hunger for each other, the perfection of their union—and not just that, he thought wonderingly, if 'just' could ever be a word applied to what they'd experienced in their intimate exploration of each other. No, 'more' was what he'd never foreseen.

The little things—the time we spend together when we are not making love. The ease of being with her. The laughter. The silences that are a tranquillity, not a strain. The companionship.

Whatever they were doing—whether it was eating under the stars or lazily lounging on the beach, or by the pool, or taking a boat out on the water, watching the sun set in a blaze of glory, or watching the moon rise through the palm trees—it was all just so...so *easy*...

And as for the sex—

His eyes flared and he felt his body tauten despite its satiation.

How could he want her so much? How could he feel what

he did—such incredible intensity every time, reaching such an incredible peak? Feel afterwards as he did now, every time, as if there was nothing more in life that he could want except to lie here with Marisa in his arms?

And he was going to have to end it. Ruin it. Destroy it.

Denounce her as the woman threatening his sister's happiness. That would end it, he knew with biting certainty. Once he had told her what his intentions for her had been all along there would be nothing left of what they had here—now.

His eyes stared at the chopping fan blades, slicing through time, slicing up his thoughts, his emotions.

I don't want to do it. I don't want to tell her, confront her, denounce her, accuse her.

But if he didn't...

He hardened his heart against himself. How could he bottle out of it? How could he put himself in front of his own sister? Put his own desires, his own longings first?

I have to do it. I don't want to but I have to. If I don't I'm just a selfish, self-indulgent coward, who cares more about myself and what I want than about my sister.

That was the brutal truth of it. The truth he couldn't deny. Couldn't hide from. He had to do it—finish what he'd started.

In his arms Marisa stirred, waking from the drowsy sleep that came after physical fulfilment. He felt her body move against him, felt himself respond. Her eyes fluttered open, met his, entwined with his. She smiled slowly, sensuously at him.

Lifted her mouth to his...

He answered her invitation, and in the velvet pleasure of her mouth he banished the disquieting thoughts that beset him.

London was far away—an ocean away.

Here, now, was all his universe.

All he wanted...

CHAPTER FOUR

MARISA sat in the taxi heading from Heathrow into central London. She looked out of the window at the bleak view beyond of the outskirts of London encased in winter's drear grip. A million miles away from the caressing warmth of the Caribbean. The grim landscape echoed the feeling inside her. In her lap, her fingers clutched each other tightly. At her side Athan had got out his laptop and was frowning at the screen, his face closed. He was only a foot or two away from her—and yet much, much further.

Tightness gripped her. She knew what was coming. Knew it with a deep, stricken sense of dread—of impending loss. Knew exactly what was going to happen. It was what she had feared would happen. He was going to escort her back to her apartment and then, in whatever way he deemed appropriate, he was going to tell her that he wouldn't be seeing her again.

The knot in her stomach tightened and her heart slugged heavily in her chest. She tried to blot out her thoughts, tried only to stare out of the window, not thinking, not feeling.

But thoughts came all the same. Of *course* Athan had been all over her while they were on holiday! Of *course* she had been the entire focus of his attention, the intensity of his desire for her would be his whole purpose. But it was only a holiday—that was what she had to remember. Nothing more than a holiday. He'd seen her, wanted her—got her. Not in any kind of exploitative way—she could never accuse him of that—but his interest in her was temporary. Inherently so. They had had a fabulous time together—but now it was over.

Time to move on.

The knot in her stomach clenched. That was the thing—*he* wanted to move on. She…she only longed for him not to. Longed for him to want to keep her in his life.

I don't want to lose him, I don't want to never see him again. I don't want it to be over!

But her wants were not going to come into it.

That was what she had to face. What she dreaded facing.

The taxi came off the flyover, threading down into the streets of London, making its way towards Shepherd's Bush, Holland Park, the street she lived on. It drew up at the apartment block. The moment it stopped she got out, shivering in the sunless cold air, acrid with the scent of the city. Athan was paying the driver, picking up their suitcases. Politely he ushered her inside and they made for the lifts. She gave another little shiver.

'It's so cold after the Caribbean,' she said, as if attempting a light remark.

Athan only smiled briefly but said nothing, not looking at her.

He would be steeling himself for his speech, she knew. How many times had he given it before? How many other women had he whisked away to paradise and then returned to earth, bidding them farewell and walking away? She felt her emotions clench, her insides hollow.

Well, what did it matter how many times before he'd done it? This would be one more time. One more *It's been good but now it's over* declamation. She hoped against hope that he wouldn't try and give her some kind of parting gift. She hoped she wouldn't cry. Hoped she would find the strength, the courage, to simply smile agreement at him and thank him for such a fabulous time together.

Part as friends.

Or just passing acquaintances.

Not that she would see him again. With his own apart-ment ready to move back into now, the rented one next door to hers would not be necessary. He'd probably already had his things moved out. Easier that way—easier to make a clean break with her.

The lift doors opened and she got out her key, opening her door while he followed with her suitcase. He set his own down in the hallway.

'Could you just leave mine in my bedroom?' she asked. Her voice was steady. Light. Deliberately so.

She went into the living room. The air in the flat was stale and chill, and she moved to the wall to turn up the thermostat. She gave another shiver, but not from the cold. Temperature reset, she turned round.

Athan was standing in the centre of the room. His expres-sion said it all. She waited tensely for him to speak. She would take it on the chin, and if nothing else behave with dignity.

I won't plead, I won't cry, I won't question. I'll just accept and move on—the way he will.

He still wasn't saying anything. He just stood there, tall, with a forbidding air about him. His face was like a mask—completely closed.

Then, abruptly, he spoke.

'I have something to say to you.'

A faint, puzzled look shadowed her eyes. His voice was so hard—so harsh. Surely he didn't have to be so hard? Wasn't there a...*civilised*...way of doing this? Of parting after a brief, incandescent affair that could not possibly last?

Did he see it in her eyes, her puzzlement, as if she were flinching a little from the severity of his tone? If he did, it only made his expression harden. The knot in Marisa's stom-ach suddenly tightened and adrenaline prickled in her veins. It was as if something bad...worse...were about to happen, and her body was steeling itself. For the first time she started to feel not just dread of him telling her it was over, but dread at something quite different…

Because what she could see in his closed, hard expression was something she had never seen there before.

It was anger.

Leashed, tightly gripped, but there. Like a force field emanating from him. She felt the dread change inside her—change into something else.

He was looking at her with eyes she'd never seen before. No flecks of gold—only bladed steel.

What is it? What's happening? Why is he being like this?

The questions flurried through her head. Bewildered apprehension showed in her eyes and her body tensed, flooded with adrenaline.

Then he struck.

'You will not be seeing Ian Randall again. You're out of his life for good.'

Shock detonated through her. He saw it in her face. Felt a savage pleasure in it. As savage as the anger that had been leashed tight within him. Now it was unleashed. He'd had to unleash it, to let it serve its purpose. An anger whose cause he would not name. Refused to name.

Because to name it would be to give it power. Power over *him.* Power he would not allow.

Could not allow…..

She clutched at the curved arm of the sofa, as if without its support she would crumple and fall. Shock was still etched across her face.

'You won't be seeing him again,' he told her. 'He's going to be working out of Athens from now on. I'm transferring him to my headquarters there.'

He'd finalised the transfer while they'd been on St Cecile—it had been the obvious thing to do, he'd realised. Get Ian out of London, keep him in Athens under his watchful and suspicious eyes. Ian Randall wouldn't be lining up any adulterous affairs under the nose of his wife's husband. Athan knew that for a certainty.

He watched how the news was going down with Marisa. His own face was still a mask. It had to be. He must not crack now—not when he'd achieved his goal. His purpose.

He had to focus on standing there, his muscles tensed. It was as if he had suddenly put on a suit of steel, banded tightly around him, keeping him motionless, immobile.

Because if he didn't—if he didn't keep his body leashed in steel—then he would surge forward, clip his arms around her, draw her to him, hold her close against him tightly, so tightly—

Marisa's expression worked—as if she were trying to cling to something, anything, that might make sense. Sense in a tidal wave of unreality...

'*You* have? But Ian doesn't work for you...'

It was a pointless thing to say—the least relevant—but the words fell from her lips all the same. Shock was ricocheting around inside her.

How does he know about Ian?

She heard him give a brief, hard laugh. There was no humour in it. Then it cut out abruptly.

'Of course he works for me.'

'No! He's marketing director of a company—'

'One of my subsidiaries.'

Her mouth opened, then closed. She had to make sense of this—somehow she had to make sense of this. She seized on the biggest thing she could not understand—out of all that she could not understand. Her mind was reeling.

'But why do you care about Ian and me? What does it matter to you, even if you do employ him indirectly? What harm is it to you?'

The questions tumbled from her—bewildered—accusatory. He felt his anger lash out again.

Anger at so much. Anger at Ian for what he was doing to Eva. Anger that he'd been landed in this mess to try and sort it out. Anger that sorting it out meant doing what he was doing now to Marisa.

I don't want to do this to her!

The thought burned across his brain. But there was no point to it. None. He had to do what he must—say what he had to. He lurched forward, his hands going around her elbows, his grip like steel.

'Because Eva Randall—' his voice was like steel wire '—Eva Randall is my sister!'

He watched her face whiten. Felt the steel bite into him, tighter yet.

'I didn't know.' Her voice was a whisper. Her eyes were distended.

He gave another harsh, humourless laugh. Because the universe was mocking him—mocking the scene he had to play out to the bitter, painful end. Because ending it was all he could do now.

'Why would he tell you?' he countered, forcing himself to speak. 'Why would he tell you what was no concern of yours? I knew he hadn't told you from the moment I introduced myself to you—the moment you saw my name on my business card. I'd gambled that he hadn't and it paid off.'

His voice changed suddenly, and as it did Marisa felt a new emotion slither through the disbelieving shock that was shaking her like an earthquake.

'Which left the field entirely clear for me. For my purpose.'

His eyes rested on her. Eyes that had once burned into her with a desire so intense she'd thought she must melt in the scorching heat of it…

Eyes that now were black like empty space. Desolate and devoid of all things.

'I sought you out,' he said, and his voice was as empty as his eyes. Saying the words he had to say. The words it would take to end it. Destroy it utterly. 'I took the apartment next door—timed my meeting with you. You'd been under my surveillance ever since I first suspected that Eva's husband was harbouring a secret. A sordid little secret. Once I'd met you I could simply put in place what had to be done. Put an end to things between you and Ian.' His voice twisted. 'After all, how could you possibly be part of his life after what you have been to me...?'

Faintness drummed at her.

From somewhere very deep inside her she found words. Each one was pulled from her like knives from wounded flesh. Costing her more than she could pay.

'It was all a set-up?'

Her eyes were huge, her face stark, skin stretched over bones, white as alabaster.

It gave her an unearthly beauty...

Anger rived through him again. Anger that she should look so beautiful.

It was a beauty he could never possess again...barred to him for ever.

'Yes,' he said. 'It was all a set-up.' He paused—a fatal pause. 'Nothing more than that.'

Nothing more than that...

The words tolled in his head like a funeral bell. Killing everything.

She was staring at him, still as a whitened corpse.

Nausea rose in her throat. 'Get out—' Her voice was a breath, a shaking rasp.

The steel bands bit into him, constricting like a crushing weight around him. He had more he had to say—must force himself to say.

'This is what you will do.' He spoke tersely, without emotion. Because emotion was far too dangerous. He had to crush it out of him. 'You will sever entirely all relations with Ian Randall. You will have nothing more to do with him. You will stay out of his life—permanently. Give him whatever reasons you want—but be aware that if you do not part from him—*permanently*—then I will give him a reason to sever relations.' He paused—another fatal pause. 'He will know what you have been to me.'

She swallowed. She could feel nausea—more than nausea—climbing in her throat. She fought it down—had to fight it down. Had to.

'Do you understand?' he demanded harshly. 'Is that clear?'

She nodded. He would not go, she knew, until he had obtained what he had come for.

What he had always planned to obtain...

No! She must not think of that—must not let the realisation of what he'd done to her explode in her brain. Not now—not yet. She stood very still, holding herself together. She was beyond speech, beyond everything.

He exhaled a sharp breath. He had done what he had set out to do. He had done it and now there was nothing else for him to do. Nothing but to do what she had told him to do—to go.

'I'll see myself out.' His voice was clipped, back in control.

He turned and walked towards the door, seizing up his suitcase from the hall beyond. His hand closed over the handle to the front door. For a moment, the barest moment, he seemed to freeze—as if...as if...

Then, abruptly, he yanked open the door and was gone.

Behind him, Marisa went on standing. Staring at where once he had been. Then slowly, very slowly, she sank down upon the sofa.

Burning with pain.

Athan strode down the corridor. His face was closed. His mind was closed. Every part of him was closed. Shut down like a nuclear reactor that had gone into meltdown and was now so dangerous only total closure could keep it from devastating all around it.

He must keep it that way. That was what was important. Essential. Keeping everything closed down.

As he descended in the lift, walked across the lobby, out into the road, reached for his mobile phone to summon a chauffeured company car to take him back to his own apartment, words went round in his head.

It's done.

That was all he had to remember.

Not Marisa at his side, his arm wrapped around her shoulder as they walked along the beach at sunset, the coral sand beneath their bare feet, the foaming wavelets washing them as they walked, and the majestic blaze of the sun sinking into the gilded azure sea.

Not Marisa beneath the stars, her beautiful swan neck stretched as she lifted her starlit face, her hair cascading like silk down her back, as he pointed out constellations to her. Not the sudden tightening in his loins as he framed her face with his hands, cupping her head, lowering his mouth to hers, lowering her body to the waiting sand beneath...

Not Marisa with her arms around him, her beauteous naked body pressed to his, crying out in ecstasy...

He wrenched his mind away, his hand around his suitcase handle clenching like steel.

He went on walking, with the biting winter all around him. Inside him.

Marisa was packing. One suitcase was packed already. She'd packed it on another continent, in another lifetime. The suitcase she was packing now was a new acquisition—one she'd bought that morning, from the nearest shop that sold luggage. Methodically, unthinkingly, she opened drawers, took out clothes, folded them into the suitcase. It didn't matter what order they went in—any order would do. It mattered only that she went on folding and packing. Folding and packing. Once the drawers were empty she moved on to the closet, performing the same office with its contents.

There were some other things as well as clothes, but those could follow later. She would box them up and have them sent on. Things like the pretty ornaments she'd acquired during her time in London, souvenirs, books, CDs. Bits and pieces.

Everything else stayed with the flat—all the kitchen goods, all the furniture, all the bedding. All she was taking were her clothes and her personal effects.

And memories.

She couldn't get rid of those. They were glued inside her head. With a glue that ate like acid into her brain.

But they were false memories. Every one of them. False because they had never happened. Because the man in the memories was not the man she had thought he was.

Her throat convulsed. Whatever her wariness over him, over what he wanted of her, she had thought she was at the least a romantic interlude for him—someone to while away a Caribbean idyll with, share a passionate affair with, enjoying their time together however transient. But she hadn't even been that. Not even that.

A lie—the whole thing had been a lie. A lie from the moment he'd asked her to keep the lift doors open for him. A set-up. Staged, managed, manipulated. Fake from the very first moment. With no purpose other than to bring her to the point she was now—cast out of Ian's life.

Because there was no going back—she knew that. She could never be any part of Ian's life now. Not even the fragile, insecure part that she had once so briefly been.

His wife is Athan's sister... Ian is his brother-in-law...

She hadn't known—hadn't guessed—hadn't suspected in a million years. And obviously Ian had not thought it necessary for her to know that his wife's brother was Athan Teodarkis, because it would mean nothing to her—why should it?

But it didn't matter, she thought tiredly. It didn't matter

who had known or not known who was what to whom. All that mattered now was that Athan Teodarkis—Ian's wife's brother—knew about her—knew what she was to Ian.

Anguish writhed inside her.

Why didn't Athan just confront me straight off? It was all he had to do. If he knew about Ian and me he could just have threatened to expose me. Why did he do what he had gone and done?

The answer was bleak and brutal. The method Athan Teodarkis had chosen was far more effective. Far more certain.

He'd been right about that. She was out of Ian's life now—and she would stay out. Nothing else was possible now. Nothing at all…

Unthinkingly, methodically, she went on with her packing.

The intercom on Athan's desk flashed repeatedly, and his secretary's voice, when she spoke, sounded flustered and apologetic.

'Kyrios Teodarkis—I am so sorry! It is Kyria Eva's husband! He insists on seeing you. I told him you had a board meeting in ten minutes, but—'

'It's all right,' Athan interrupted her. 'I'll see him.' His voice was grim. So was his expression. He had half expected this. Ian Randall would not lightly give up his intended mistress.

Who would give up Marisa Milburne? So beautiful, so passionate a woman.

The familiar guillotine sliced down over his thoughts. It had been much in use these past days. Slicing down ruthlessly on so many thoughts—so many memories. But he would allow himself none of them—not a single one. Their indulgence was forever barred to him. His eyes hardened. He would not allow his feckless, faithless brother-in-law to indulge himself any longer with his forbidden fruit.

I had to give her up—so must he!

His expression was still reflecting the savagery of his thoughts as Ian swept in. He looked agitated and launched straight in.

'Athan—what the hell is this about? Neil Mackay says it comes from you, but I don't understand why. Why do you want me at your HQ?'

Athan sat back. He appeared unperturbed by the outburst. 'It's time you moved on. And up. It's promotion, Ian—aren't you pleased?'

His tone was equable. He would keep this civil—or his sister would get wind of a fracas between him and her husband and get upset.

'Oh, come on,' Ian said disbelievingly. 'You've no call to promote me!' He paused, eyes narrowing. 'This is about Eva, isn't it? You think it will please her to be back in Athens.'

Athan's gaze levelled on him. 'Eva's happiness is paramount to me.' He paused. 'Never forget that.' He paused again, and when he spoke, it carried the message he intended it to. 'After all—' his voice was limpid '—it was because it made her happy that I let her marry you.'

Colour mounted in his brother in law's face. 'And you've never forgiven me for marrying her, have you?'

Athan's gaze never dropped. 'Providing you don't hurt her, or upset her, I…tolerate you.'

He watched glacially as the colour flared out across his brother-in-law's handsome face. The face of a man who helped himself to whatever he wanted in life—smiling, charming, selfish, self-indulgent. He'd charmed Eva, wooed her, and ended up persuading her to marry him.

And proved himself faithless within two years of their wedding.

Silently Athan cursed his unwanted brother-in-law. Cursed the life-long intimacy between their families—Sheila Randall's all-but-adoption of his then teenaged sister.

He cursed Sheila's son for getting anywhere near the impressionable, vulnerable Eva so disastrously eager to fall in love with his golden looks and easy charm.

Cursed him for having used those same golden looks and easy charm to work their damage on yet another woman—on Marisa...

'You...*tolerate* me?' Ian's voice cut through his litany of inner curses.

'That's very good of you, Athan. Very...generous. But maybe—' now there was something different in his voice that made Athan's eyes narrow '—maybe I'm tired of your tolerance. Tired of your generosity. Tired of it being known that as Athan Teodarkis's brother-in-law no wonder I'm a board director, no wonder I get sent off on plush secondments to the West Coast, with instructions to take holidays in Hawaii to keep my wife happy—my boss's sister.' He took a step forward. 'Maybe it's time to tell you I can live without your *tolerance,* your generosity!'

Athan's gaze skewered him. 'And maybe—' his voice cracked like a whip, all civility gone now '—you'll do *exactly* what I say you will. Or would you rather—' he bit out each word '—I tell Eva about Marisa Milburne.'

Ian Randall froze. Before Athan's eyes the other man's face paled. 'How the hell do you know about Marisa?' he demanded.

Athan spread his hands out on his desk. 'Don't take me for an idiot. You installed her in a flat in Holland Park.'

'You bastard,' Ian breathed. 'You spied on me.'

'Like I said—don't take me for an idiot.' Athan's voice was caustic.

'And you would actually be prepared to tell Eva about her?' Ian said in a hollow tone.

Athan's lasering gaze never left his brother-in-law's face. 'I won't have to. Marisa Milburne is no longer in your flat.'

'*What?*'

'You heard me. She's gone. Cleared out.' He paused. 'Presumably,' he said deliberately, his eyes like slate, 'she's selected another wealthy lover to beguile...?'

He saw Ian's face freeze again. But this time there was something in his frozen gaze that Athan could not identify. Then slowly, as if the ice was thawing, his brother-in-law turned and headed for the door. As he reached it, he turned. His face was like marble.

'You'll have my letter of resignation on your desk tomorrow morning.'

Then he was gone.

Almost, Athan charged after him. Charged after him to seize his shoulders and shake him like the rat he was. But he wouldn't soil himself on the man. As for his threatened resignation—he'd never do it. The position he had was far too cushy a number. And if he tried to go it alone, escape from Athan's scrutiny—*necessary* scrutiny, as he'd amply demonstrated—Eva would kick up. She wouldn't want any bad feeling between her husband and her brother.

Grimly, Athan made himself sit back in his chair, his face like thunder. Let Ian rush out and vent his spleen! Do whatever the hell he wanted. Anger bit through him. Damn the man—damn him and double damn him!

Angrily, he swung in his chair, his eyes stormy, unforgiving. If Eva's philandering husband had had the slightest moral backbone Marisa Milburne would never now be plaguing him the way she was.

Never haunting him the way she was.

Filling his memory. Tormenting him.

Tormenting him with wanting her. That was the damnation of it—the thing he was trying to crush out of his mind, his memory. Because what was the point of letting it torment him? There was nothing he could do about it—nothing. He had to accept that. He'd decided on his strategy to ensure that his wretched, faithless brother-in-law would be severed from the woman who had beguiled him, and now he had to abide by the consequences of that strategy.

But I didn't think it would be like this.

That was the devil of it. He'd never for a moment imagined that he'd be left feeling like this.

Cheated. That was the word. The emotion. Cheated of a woman who'd turned out to be someone not just easy to seduce but...memorable. Memorable in so many ways. All of them incredible.

Cheated... The word twisted in his head again. He knew it was a pointless word—a pointless emotion for him to feel. He'd gone into this with his eyes open, his mind made up, his strategy planned and flawlessly executed. He had succeeded completely, achieved his aim, finished his mission. It should be the end of the story. It was—for her and Ian. But not for him.

I still want her. I want her, and I don't want it to be the end. I want to have her back again

I can't. It's as simple as that—and as brutal. I seduced her to take her away from Ian—not for myself. It was never about her, it was only about Eva.

Moodily, he stared ahead of him, seeing not his plush office but the silver sand beach, the swaying palms, the turquoise sea. And Marisa.

Always Marisa.

Tormenting him.

Slowly, Marisa climbed out of the taxi and handed the driver the fare. It was a horribly large amount, and in her pre-Ian days she would never have dreamt of taking a taxi from the railway station some twenty miles away. She would have waited for the local bus, which ran four times a day and no more, and then got out at the village and walked the remaining mile up to the cottage. But now she could afford the luxury of a taxi from the station—all thanks to Ian.

But she mustn't think about Ian. Not now. Ian belonged to a world she had never been part of—not even on the fringes, where she had clung. Athan Teodarkis had prised her from where she had been so hopelessly clinging. She should be glad of it—glad that he had shown her with callous brutality just how much she was not any part of that world.

She looked about her as the taxi turned around and headed back down the narrow lane, out of sight. She shivered. Winter still clutched the land, making the air clammy with cold, and the bare trees shivered in the chill wind that blew off the moor. It was dank and drear, and the late afternoon was losing its light, closing down the day. In front of her the cottage looked forlorn and ramshackle. A slate had come loose, she could see, and water dripped from a leaf-blocked gutter. The garden looked sodden, with the remnants of last autumn's leaves turned a mushy brown on the pathway to the front door.

With a heavy sigh and a heavier heart she heaved up her suitcases and the bag of groceries she'd bought and opened the creaking wooden gate. She walked up to the front door. As it opened to her key the smell of damp assailed her. Inside was colder than outside. She gave another shiver, set down her cases, and went through to the kitchen with the carrier bag. The ancient range was stone-cold, not lit since the day she had left for London months before. The cob walls and small windows made it darker than ever, and she turned on the electric light—which only showed up the dust on the kitchen table, illuminated the dead flies on the windowsill.

Depression closed around her like a cold, tight blanket. Numbly, she went about the tasks required to make the cottage habitable: turning on the fridge and putting the fresh food away in it, relighting the range, wiping down the dusty surfaces, trying to keep her mind on the mundane tasks, not on anything else. Not on the empty dreariness of the cottage, on the bleakness in her heart.

The cottage was so empty—so absolutely and totally

empty. Grief filled her—grief for the mother no longer there, her absence palpable. Grief for Ian, whose life she could no longer be even the barest part of.

And grief for something else—something that she dared not allow lest it consume her.

Overwhelmed, she felt her throat tightening, the emotion welling up inside her, and she sank down on one of the kitchen chairs, her head sinking on her folded arms. Hot, shaking sobs filled her. She cried out all her loneliness, all her grief. And one more emotion too. Fiercer, sharper—like a needle flashing in and out of her, over and over again, weaving through her in a thousand piercings. Questions, accusations—self-accusations—tumbled about in her. Jumbled and jostled and fought for air.

How could he do that to me? How could I fall for it? How can it hurt so much? How can it matter so much? How could I mind so much?

How, how, how...?

Anguish consumed her. Why had he not simply confronted her and told her she must have nothing more to do with Ian? Been up-front, honest—brutal from the start?

Not at the end. Not after luring her with soft words, false smiles...

False kisses...

And more, far more than kisses.

She lifted her head, staring sightlessly out over the kitchen. Once so familiar to her, now it was like an alien landscape. In front of her was not the cottage with its thick cob walls, its old fashioned cupboards and furniture, the smell of damp and mustiness.

Heat and blazing sun, and the lapping of azure waters, the feel of the sand beneath her feet and her heart full.

She felt her lungs tighten as though they must burst.

How could he do it to me? How?

How was it possible that he should been able to take

her in his arms, make love to her, and all the while it was just some cruel, calculating manoeuvre to get her out of his brother-in-law's life?

Her tears dried on her cheeks, leaving dampened runnels and her expression like stone.

He deceived me from the very first—fooled me and conned me and lied to me. Lied in word and deed.

Grimly she stared blindly ahead. Lies, lies, lies. Foul, deceiving lies. Smiling while he lied. Kissing her while he lied. Making love to her while he lied.

She jumped to her feet as if to banish all the hot, angry, anguished thoughts from her head. Nothing could change what had happened. It was as if she'd swallowed a snake— a poisonous snake that was now biting at her with its fangs inside, injecting its venom into her blood.

Angrily she strode through the narrow corridor to the front door, seizing up her suitcases, and heading up the creaking stairs to her old bedroom. It was freezing upstairs, and the smell of damp prevailed. But what did she care? What did she care about anything any more?

He can go to hell! Go to hell and stay there!

Hatred seared through her as venomous as the poison in her veins, seeking only one target—Athan Teodarkis. The man who had brought her to this. Taken her to paradise— and then smashed her into the ground.

CHAPTER FIVE

'ATHAN—what's happening? What's going on?'

Eva's voice down the phone line from London sounded strained. Athan could hear the anxiety in it, the worry, and cursed inwardly.

'Ian won't explain—won't tell me anything. But you and he have fallen out, haven't you? I know you have.'

He took a breath and put on his most calming voice—the one he used to try and reassure her when she got stressed over things. 'I don't want you worrying—' he began.

She cut across him, her voice rising in pitch. 'How can I possibly not worry? I'm worried sick! My husband comes home and announces he's resigned from his job! That he won't work for you any more. Athan, what have you said to him? Why is he doing this?'

Athan's hand around the phone receiver tightened. Ian had stormed out like a damn drama queen because he'd been shown up for the adulterous rat he was. But that was the last thing that Eva could ever know. Athan's teeth ground together angrily. And to protect her he had to protect her husband's dirty little secret.

'Eva, it isn't like that,' he said soothingly. 'It was a mutual decision,' he lied. 'Ian's made it clear to me for some time that he's restless, that he wants to quit.'

'But *why?* I was so thrilled that you trusted him enough to take him on board!'

Athan rolled his eyes, glad his sister couldn't see his expression. It wasn't because he trusted Ian Randall that he'd taken him on. The complete reverse! It was because he'd wanted to keep him where he could see him—where he would have to toe the line. His mouth thinned. And that was just what he hadn't done—and now Ian thought he could evade control by doing a runner.

Eva must not see it like that, though—that was essential. So he had to lie, to smooth it down, play it down.

'I guess he felt a bit overpowered, Eva,' he said. 'It's natural that he wants to try his wings out on his own—prove his own mettle. It could even be that he's been head-hunted,' he ventured placidly. 'After all, a stint at one of the Teodarkis companies makes Ian very employable.'

His efforts to placate his sister, to assure her that her husband's desertion was not a bad thing and did not indicate any falling out with his brother-in-law seemed to be working. Eva seemed to be calming down.

'Well, I suppose that's true,' she said, her voice steadying and losing the nervous tension that had racked it when she'd first spoken. 'But I was scared that he'd walked out because he'd quarrelled with you. You know he's in awe of you, Athan.' Her voice sounded sad. 'I just want you and him to get on well together, that's all.'

Athan said nothing. There were some things he couldn't lie about. Like the fact that nothing could make him 'get on well' with the man who had married his sister against all his instinctive disapproval of the match. His sister deserved so much better than a philandering lightweight like Ian Randall.

As for what the man would do now—Athan had no idea. He'd trotted out that line about Ian being highly employable but he had no great belief in it. He knew perfectly well that others assumed Ian Randall held his prestigious position as director of marketing at one of the key subsidiaries within the Teodarkis organisation purely because his brother-in-law

owned the company. He wouldn't pick up another plum position like that out in the open market. No, without the shelter
that he'd got from his brother-in-law Ian would find the corporate world a much harsher place. He might have enjoyed
himself, storming out of his office, but reality would soon
hit home. Athan's lip curled. He'd take pleasure in seeing Ian
come crawling back for his old job.

He gave an exasperated sigh. He'd get it, too—because
Eva would be upset otherwise. In the meantime—well, Ian
Randall could just stay out of his hair or do anything else he
damn well liked.

With one exception.

He would not go anywhere near Marisa Milburne.

So far he hadn't, and Athan intended it to stay that way.
He didn't believe Ian would try, now that he knew that his
brother-in-law knew about her, but he wasn't taking chances.
On the other hand job-hunting should, Athan profoundly
hoped, keep Ian's mind off his intended mistress—*former*
intended mistress, he reminded himself grimly—at least for
the time being.

He sighed heavily.

*I have to get over her! I have to put her away, in the past,
and not let myself think about her or remember her and the
time we had together. It's over—gone, finished. She's out of
Ian's life—out of mine.*

For good.

But it was one thing to adjure himself to forget Marisa—to
refuse to let himself go back down those tempting, dangerous
pathways of his mind—quite another to achieve it. He stared
out over the Athens skyline. Where was she now? he found
himself thinking. She'd cleared out of London—out of the
apartment Ian Randall had paid for—and gone. That was all
he cared about—all he could allow himself to care about. The
fact that she had disappeared. Disappeared as swiftly as she

had appeared. Had she left London altogether? Or just gone to live somewhere else in the city?

Had she found another man? Another lover?

An image, hot and tormenting, leapt in his mind's eye.

Marisa in another man's arms—another man's bed...

He thrust it out of his head, refused to let it back in. It was nothing to him—*nothing!*—whether or not she'd found another man to fill her life with. That was all he must remember—all he must allow himself to think.

Grimly he crossed to his drinks cabinet, yanking open the doors. Maybe a shot of alcohol would banish the image from his head. Give him the peace he sought.

I need another woman.

The crudity of his thought shocked him, but that, he knew, was what it boiled down to. There was only one way to get Marisa Milburne out of his consciousness and that was by replacing her in it. He took a heavy intake of breath. OK, so how about starting right now? He could fill every evening with a hectic social life if he wanted—and right now that seemed like a good idea. A whole lot better than resorting to alcohol, for a start.

Shutting the drinks cabinet doors again, he strode from the room.

An hour later, changed from lounge suit to dinner jacket, he was mouthing polite nothings in a crowded salon at a cocktail party, wondering whether he needed his head examined. At least three women, each of them stunningly beautiful, were vying for his attention, and he was trying to give none of them reason to think he was favouring any of them. None of them, nor any of the other women at the party, had the slightest allure for him. Even after a second glass of vintage champagne.

Restlessly he looked about him, hoping against hope that someone, somewhere, would catch his eye. But as his gaze ran over the assembled females dispassionately not a single one made him look twice.

'…in the Caribbean…'

The fragment of speech brought him back. One of the women—a voluptuous brunette with lush lips and a traffic-stopping figure—was talking, it seemed, about a proposed cruise. She was pausing invitingly for him to say something.

But he wasn't seeing her…

He was seeing Marisa leaning against him, curled up beside him on the wide palanquin-style sun-shelter in front of their cabana, overlooking the beach, sipping a cocktail with him as they watched the sun go down in a blaze of gold and crimson. Her body so soft, so warm nestled against him. Her pale hair was like a golden rope down the backless sundress she was wearing. His mouth was brushing the satin of her hair, his hand cupped her shoulder, holding her close… so close.

The warmth of her body—the sweetness of its scent—the heady longing of desire, of possession, wrapping them together.

His mouth nuzzled at her cheekbone. She turned her face to his, caught his lips with hers, let him draw her down upon the soft, yielding surface…

'What do you think?'

The brightly voiced enquiry roused him painfully, and he had to refocus his eyes, his mind. 'Is a cruise around the Caribbean a good idea? Or is it better to be based on land?'

He gave an absent half smile. 'I guess it depends how vulnerable you are to seasickness,' he answered, hoping it was a suitable answer in a conversation he had paid no attention to.

'Oh, I get *horribly* seasick,' one of the other women contributed, and turned her eyes full-on to Athan. 'There are so many gorgeous islands. Which one do you recommend? St Bart's? Martinique? Barbados—though that is *so* over-popular now, alas!'

He answered at random. His thoughts were far away, across the ocean, on the only Caribbean island he cared about. St Cecile. The one that held all his memories of Marisa.

I want her back.

The words formed in his head before he could stop them. Burning and indelible.

He wanted Marisa back. That was all there was to it. Simple, and straight to the point.

I don't care who she is—what she was to Ian—why I did what I did. I just want her back. I don't care how impossible it is.

He had finally admitted it. Faced up to and acknowledged the truth he'd been trying to deny ever since he'd stalked out of her apartment, having told her that everything between them had been a set-up—a lie.

But he could deny the truth no longer. He wanted Marisa back again…

But I can't—it's impossible. Out of the question. It's the most damn out-of-the-question thing in the world!

He had to put it out of his head. Put *her* out. Whatever it took. He looked anew at the bevy of beautiful women dancing attendance on him. He had come here tonight to this glittering social gathering, to where he was a familiar face, the Athenian high society circuit, with the specific purpose of finding another woman to take his mind off the one he couldn't have. But the problem was he didn't want any of them. Not a single one.

Dispassionately he assessed them, and those around him in the ornate salon. Even those not blessed with natural beauty were wearing *haute couture* numbers, shimmering with expensive jewellery, coiffed and manicured to the nines, looking fabulous and elegant whatever their age. Yet not one of them appealed.

Marisa could float in with just with a towel wrapped round her, not a scrap of make up and her hair in a ponytail, and she would still be the only woman I want.

With a heavy, self-accusing sigh at his own hopeless weakness, he rejoined the conversation. It was not the fault of the women here that he didn't want them. At the very least he owed them courtesy and attention.

Somehow he got through the remainder of the evening until he felt he could bid his hostess goodbye and finally beat a retreat. Back in his own apartment, glad to be on his own again at last, he went out on to the balcony. Though it was still chilly, winter was over now. Spring would be blessing the land again soon, and then the heat of the Aegean summer. For now he welcomed the cool—welcomed looking out over the Athens skyline, polluted though the air was, and thinking his own thoughts.

OK, he reasoned, for a change marshalling his brainpower to a purpose, not of corporate affairs or the economic problems besetting the world, but to his own dilemma. He had to be blunt about this. He wanted a woman it was impossible to have. Impossible because it would damage his family, jeopardise his sister's shaky marriage. Having anything more to do with the woman who had nearly destroyed it was unthinkable.

Yet when he had tried to divert his attention to another woman—any woman!—he had found to his dismay that he might as well have been gazing at a cardboard cut-out.

There was, therefore, only one solution. It was staring him in the face, but it wasn't one he was particularly attracted to. But still there it was.

Celibacy.

Going without.

Abstinence.

He took a heavy breath. It would be hard, but it was his only option right now. Somehow he had to purge the last influences of Marisa Milburne from him, and living like a monk was his only effective method. And what he would have to do in order to ensure that he could achieve that purging was refuse to think about her, remember her, long for her. He'd fill his head up with other stuff.

Work would be good 'other stuff'…

He gazed out bleakly, glimpsing the ancient rock of the Acropolis crowned with the ruins of the Parthenon. A temple to Athena. The patroness of Athens. A virgin goddess. The goddess of wisdom and fortitude.

He would need both those qualities in quantity from now on.

Marisa watched the dark blue car wind its way slowly down the narrow lane from the cottage back towards the village and the road beyond that led out of Devon, back towards the motorway that headed for London. Her heart was heavy and torn, but she had done the right thing—she knew she had.

Ian had pleaded with her, but she had held firm—cost her though it had.

I had to do it—I had to convince him that I just can't be part of his life any more. Not now—not ever.

He had arrived, despite all her pleas to him by text and phone not to, that morning. He had been aghast that she had moved out of the flat in London he'd leased for her, begged her to reconsider, change her mind—come back.

But of course she couldn't. Wouldn't. Athan Teodarkis had made that impossible. Unthinkable.

Going back to her old home, her old life, was the only thing that was possible. Here at the very least she could hide. Hide from everything—and everyone. Ian insisting on confronting her here had been an ordeal, but draining though it had been, and upsetting, she knew that it had had to be done to convince him she'd made her decision and was going to stick to it. So now—painfully—he'd gone, leaving the knowledge that she could not possibly tell him what his brother-in-law had done to her burning inside her like acid.

As she watched Ian's car disappear around the curve of the lane she shut her eyes, feeling a kind of relief at his departure that was at odds with the wrench of watching him leave her life. She felt breathless and suffocated by all the emotion pressing down upon her. On an impulse she went back inside the cottage and changed her indoor shoes for a stout, well-worn pair of ankle boots, grabbed an anorak and the cottage keys, and headed out of the back door.

A pathway led from the garden up through the last of the fields below the moor, then broke free onto the moorland itself. It was a cloudy day, with a westerly wind sending the clouds scudding, and drops of rain shaking down from time to time. But the weather didn't matter—only getting out of the cottage. It was a familiar walk—she'd done it a thousand times in her youth. Sometimes with her mother, sometimes on her own. It had always given her refreshment. There was something about the moorland, up above the farmed fields, directly under the sky, that opened her up, let out the feelings and emotions that troubled and oppressed her—whatever those troubles and oppressions were.

And now she was walking here again, into the wild air, across the infertile land where only heather and gorse and rough grass flourished, up across the uneven, curving terrain towards the distant tor—the granite outcrop that loomed on the horizon.

It took an hour of brisk walking to get there, and she was out of condition after all her time in London, but she got there in the end and found her familiar nook amongst the rocks, sitting herself down on a horizontal shelf of granite, facing out over the vast expanse of moorland beyond. The westerly wind keened over the land and through the gaps in the rocks, winnowing her face. Rain blew in on the wind, but her cheeks were already wet—wet with the tears she was shedding.

Tears for so much. For her mother, who had been deprived of the love and happiness she'd sought, and who'd had to make do with a constricted, unfulfilled life here when she'd once hoped for so much more.

Just like I did—so short a time ago.

But those hopes had been crushed and brutally exposed for the folly they always had been.

I should have known that I could never be part of Ian's life—never be accepted, never tolerated.

She gazed bleakly over the bare landscape. Her mother had warned her—warned her about the world she sought—but she hadn't believed her, hadn't wanted to believe her. Her mother had been burnt, too, expelled and rejected, and that was why she'd sought refuge here, in this lonely place, accepting a life austere and alone, instead of the life she had once hoped for.

Her mother's hopes had been cruelly dashed.

So, now, had her own.

Marisa's eyes darkened. She had had days now to try and accept what Athan had done to her—to join together the two utterly different people he seemed to be, to accept that the man she'd thought she'd known, the man she'd come to trust, to give herself to, had been nothing like that at all.

Ruthless. Brutal. Lethal.

That was the true Athan Teodarkis. That was the man she had to see him as. No matter what dreams came in the night, beguiling her. No matter what memories tried to seep into her consciousness, tormenting her.

She lifted her face into the wind, the oncoming rain. Her hair was plastered to her head but she didn't care. She was used to the weather—glad of the punishing elements battering her. She deserved them to be lashing her.

I was a fool—a trusting, self-deceiving fool—who fell for a man who was all surface, all temptation...

Just as her mother had done.

The realisation hit her like an intake of breath. She shut

her eyes, rocking with the ugly, accusing truth of it. The pain of recognition scalded her.

Her mother had been a fool once, hoping for her dreams to come true—but she'd founded her hopes on a man who had made a fool of her.

Just as Athan has made a fool of me...

Pain seized her. Racking her body. She forced herself to be still, to wait it out, to let it pass. She'd been doing that for days now, every time the memory of that nightmare conversation in the apartment leapt to malevolent, vicious life in her head—his denouncement of her, telling her that he'd set up everything between them for the sole purpose of separating her from Ian.

The last of the louring clouds passed overhead and sunshine, bright through the rain-washed air, pooled over her. It was pale and had hardly any heat in it—a frail, fleeting lightening of the grim, bleak day.

Not like the hot, fierce sun of the Caribbean, beating down on my bare shoulders like a physical force, soaking into me as I lay on a sun lounger, idly chatting to Athan lying beside me. Filtering through the louvered windows when we retired to our cabana after lunch to make love...

The pain came again, but she quenched it. Quenched it by will power, by the power of the shame that she had fallen for such a ruthless, heartless masquerade. Because, whatever the rights and wrongs of it, he had lied to her from the very start, and nothing—not the slightest thing about him—had been true.

She got to her feet, scrambling down from her perch in the rocks of the tor and jumping down onto the wet ground. She paused to gaze around her at the vast expanse of open moor. On a rise a few hundred yards away she could see the low outline of stone-edged walls, almost obliterated by heather and time. It was a Bronze Age village, thousands of years old, and it was a familiar part of the landscape to her.

Now, as she looked across at it, she wondered at the people who had once, so very long ago, lived there, made their lives there. They had loved and lived and worked and died, each little life as important to its owner as hers was to her. Yet all there was left of them was a few stones.

My life will be like that one day. Leaving not even a shadow on the land. So what does it matter if I am hurt or humiliated or angry or anguished? Soon the pain I feel will pass—soon I will feel nothing.

It had been true for her mother, surely, that a time had come when the man who had treated her so badly no longer had the power to wound her?

I'll make it true of me, too. I have to.

Slowly, she made her way back down off the moor. The sunshine remained, thin and pale, but better than the rain. The wind was softer here, in the lee of the moor, and there was the scent of spring in it. Winter was nearly over.

All she needed was time. Time to let him fade like a bad dream, to let him go, to move on, forward into a life that she was yet to make. What that new life would be she didn't know—couldn't even envisage. She had thought when she'd left the cottage to go to London that her life was just starting—now she was stranded back here again, with no way forward that she could think of.

But I'll find one—I can. I must. And I can be strong—I have to!

Resolution filled her. With a firmer step she headed down the trackway that led off the moor, climbing the stile that gave on to the dead end of the lane that went back past her cottage to the village a mile or so beyond. The light was fading now, the sun sunk below the tor behind her, and she wanted to get back to the cottage before evening closed in. But as she rounded the final bend of the narrow lane she stopped short.

A car was parked in front of the cottage. For a moment she thought it must be Ian, returning despite her refusal to go back to London with him, but then she realised it was another make of car, and even in the dusk she could see the colour was different. It was an expensive car, though, as Ian's had been—sleek and powerful-looking. But it wasn't until the driver's door opened that she realised just who had come to call…

Athan unfolded his tall frame from the confines of the car he'd been sitting in since his arrival half an hour ago, and watched Marisa walk towards him. His emotions were tamped down—under strict control. They had been ever since he'd got the phone call from his security agency—the call he'd been steeling himself against, hoping he would never get it. But, as predictable as a greedy child stealing from the candy jar, Ian Randall had done exactly what Athan had feared he would do.

Icily he'd heard out the phone call, taking in the bare, bald details provided. Time, route, venue. It was all he'd needed to know. Now, though, he needed to know a hell of a lot more…

She walked up to him. She had nerve, he gave her that. Or perhaps it was her lover's presence that was giving her confidence. Not that there was any sign of Ian, or his car.

His voice, harsh and rough, cut through the chilly air.

'Where is he?' It was a curt demand, and he wanted an answer.

She stopped dead. Absently, Athan wondered at her appearance. She looked totally different from the way he was used to seeing her. She had a baggy pair of trousers on, mud-spattered boots, and a voluminous anorak that was as unflattering as it was obscuring of her figure. Her hair was sopping wet, and dragged back off her head with a clip. She looked a sodden mess.

But her face—her face was as breathtaking as ever. Her eyes, flashing with anger, were luminous, her mouth kissed by the rain…

'He's gone.' Her voice was as curt as his. She knew exactly who Athan meant. Knew exactly why he was here. Anger spiked in her, because it was obvious that the only way Athan Teodarkis could have known where his brother-in-law had gone was if he'd had him tailed.

'Didn't your spies spot him heading back to London?' she threw at him caustically.

Athan's face tightened. No, they hadn't—or at least he hadn't had a report to that effect. He'd told them to keep a discreet distance—presumably it had been too discreet. But even so the point was clear. Despite everything he'd said to Ian, the man had still come chasing after his mistress like a dog on heat…

He strode towards her.

She flinched, but held her ground. Shock waves were detonating through her, but she had to ignore them. Had to ignore more than just the shock of seeing Athan Teodarkis, tall, forbidding and grim-visaged, here outside her home. The juxtaposition was jarring. Athan Teodarkis didn't belong here in this rural backwater, in this bleak, stark landscape dripping with the dregs of winter. But, however jarring, it was not that which was consuming her self-control.

Emotions were hurtling through her—tumbling and overwhelming her.

Athan! Athan here—now! Right in front of her! So close… his presence overpowering her senses.

She almost reeled from the impact of it.

I didn't think I would ever see him again!

But he was here, and she could feel her treacherous blood leaping in her veins, emotion pouring through her…

She had to subdue it—had to make herself realise that he was here for one reason and one reason only. Because Ian had come to her. That was all. That was why he was here—angry. Accusing.

But this time her conscience was clear. His accusations could reach no target—none.

'So whatever you think you're doing here—you can clear off!' she said. 'He isn't here.'

His eyes narrowed—eyes that had once looked at her with hot, melting desire…now filled only with cold anger.

'But he came here all the same.'

Her chin lifted. 'And now he's gone—for good.'

Athan stilled. 'Did you tell him about us?'

Marisa's lip curled in scorn. 'Of course I didn't.'

No, thought Athan, *of course you didn't. You wouldn't want him to know how easily I seduced you…took you away from him.*

He smiled in grim satisfaction. His anger was ebbing now. Anger fuelled by much more than fury at his philandering brother in law. Fuelled by a far more powerful impulse. The impulse that had brought him here, powering down the motorway relentlessly, as driven as the car bringing him here. Driven by a force he could no longer suppress—no longer wanted to suppress.

He nodded at the cottage. 'I need to talk to you—and not out here.' He stamped his feet. His Italian leather handmade shoes were fine for the city. Not fine for a cold evening in the wilds.

'I've got nothing to say to you.' Marisa's voice was still curt. Shock was still detonating through her.

He looked at her. In the dusk his expression was saturnine. 'But I,' he told her, 'have something to say to *you.*' His expression changed slightly. 'You look frozen,' he said.

For a moment the breath caught in her throat. There had been concern in his voice—caring.

The way he'd once sounded when he spoke to her…

Brutal truth sliced down, forcing open her throat. He'd lied to her from the beginning—lied with every caring, affectionate, casual word. That was what she must remember.

Not the way he used to look at her—the way his mouth

would quirk with that half smile of his, the way his dark, lam-
bent eyes used to rest on her...

She cut off the memory again. No, not that way at all.

She shivered under the anorak. He was right—she felt frozen. Stiffly she went up to the front door and opened it with
the key taken from the map pocket in her anorak. He followed
her in. Immediately the small cottage felt smaller. She didn't
want to let him in—didn't want him here. Didn't want him
anywhere near her within a thousand miles.

Liar! Liar—liar—liar!

The words in her head accused her, betrayed her. Again
she had to call on the cold, emotionless self-control she'd
faced him with outside the cottage. It didn't matter where he
was—he was nothing to her. The same nothing to her that
she was to him.

She would let him say whatever it was he had to say—another reinforcement about her staying out of Ian's life was all
it could be—and then she would send him packing. He could
find his own way back to the village, his own way back to the
motorway. What did she care? Nothing—that was what she
cared. All that was left of her feelings for him...

Nothing.

She went into the kitchen, feeling relief at the warmth from
the wood range enveloping her. Shrugging off her wet anorak,
she draped it around one of the chairs at the scrubbed wooden
kitchen table and opened the door to the range, restacking it
with wood. Then she filled the kettle and set it on one of the
rings to boil. Familiar tasks that gave her hands and brain
something to do while she tried to assimilate the fact—jolt-
ing, bizarre, impossible—that Athan Teodarkis had sat himself down at the kitchen table in a tiny cob-walled cottage
that had been a haven for her mother after the ruination of
her happiness.

Her gaze went to the man sitting at her kitchen table who
could reach out with a single finger and with a single touch

melt her like honey. Who could quirk a slanting smile at her and weaken her bones. Who could wind his hand around the nape of her neck and lower his mouth to hers, and take her to a paradise she had never dreamt of...

A man who had never—not once until that bitter, scathing denouement—said an honest word to her.

She took a breath. 'You said you had something to say—so say it. Say it and go.'

Gimlet eyes snapped to her. He'd been looking around him, taking in the room they were in. It had come as a shock to him, seeing how poor a place it was.

No wonder the world Ian moved in had seemed so tempting to her—no wonder she'd been so impressed by him, beguiled by him. Coming from a place like this, to her Ian's world must have seemed glittering and luxurious beyond anything she could have hoped for.

It sobered him. He couldn't deny it.

His gaze went back to her. His mind split instantly into two. One half was taking in just how shabby she looked—the other was simply drinking her in like a thirsty man in a desert. Even without a scrap of make-up, with wet, stringy hair and atrocious clothes, she still made his pulse leap!

'Well?'

Her voice refocused him. 'Do you need any money?' The question came out more bluntly than he'd intended. Nor was it the question he'd wanted to ask her—but after seeing this rundown place it had come out of his mouth without thinking.

'What?'

Athan looked slightly awkward. He really hadn't meant to sound that blunt, but it was too late now. He took a breath.

'Look, I've got eyes in my head. I can see there's one hell of a difference between your lifestyle in London and what you've got here. So, if you need something to tide you over I can easily—'

He got no further. She slammed the mug she'd been about to fill with coffee down on to the wooden table.

'No! I do *not* want your stinking money!' Her eyes were like lasers, and he had to shield himself from their glare.

'It was an offer—nothing more than that.' He had to mitigate. 'If Ian's seen you all right then you won't need anything from me.'

'You'll be glad to know,' she said, as sweetly as acid, 'that Ian does not continue to fund me.'

'I'm glad to hear it,' he said evenly, taking the fight back to her. 'And it's just as well—he is about to become unemployed. No,' he said, holding up a hand to silence her, 'it was not my doing. He's resigned from the company.' He paused. 'He didn't tell you?'

Marisa was looking pale. 'No. But…but why?'

Athan spelt it out, keeping his gaze on her to assess her reaction. 'He wishes to cut the apron strings from me. Assert his independence. Which is why,' he went on, his voice tinged with sarcasm, 'you will doubtless understand my concern that he has high-tailed it down to find you. I don't want him thinking he is now free to take up with you again.'

'Well, he isn't, is he?' she retorted. 'You've seen to that. How can I possibly look him in the face knowing what his own brother-in-law did to me?'

'Indeed,' Athan's voice was smooth now. 'So—' he took a breath '—he's accepted he cannot see you again? You told him that? Made it crystal-clear?'

'Yes.' Her monosyllabic reply was clipped, unemotional. But her emotions were running all the same—like a deep, underground river, cutting through the rocks and obstacles in her mind. Obstacles she had to keep in place. Absolutely had to…

'Good.'

He sounded satisfied. But there was something in his voice that alarmed her. It was not the satisfaction of a man who had disposed of an embarrassing and unwanted family problem.

'In which case...' he said, his eyes resting on her. 'In which case,' he repeated, 'I have something else to say to you.'

She stared. Her heart-rate had started to quicken, but she didn't want it to. As she didn't want to see what she was seeing in his eyes.

He's too close. This kitchen is too small. I can't breathe—can't find fresh air...

He was still sitting at the kitchen table, but his presence dominated the room—dominated her senses, her vision. She tried to think straight, but she couldn't. Everything about him focussed her on *him,* and deep within her still that powerful subterranean river of emotion was coursing, seeking its way upwards, out of the depths of her mind...

'It's this.'

He was speaking again, and she heard his words—heard the accent in them that had so worked on her, drawn her to him, just as everything about him had drawn her hopelessly, ineluctably, irresistibly...

His sloe-dark eyes were resting on her, delving into her, winding her gaze on his like a spool, so she could only look back at him, her eyes widening, melting...

'I want you back.'

His words fell into the space between them. The space that would soon no longer be between them...

Because it was quite clear in his head now. Crystal-clear. It had taken till this morning to crystallise—and it had done so instantly, irreversibly, when his phone had rung and he'd been told that Ian Randall was heading down to Devon.

In that instant he'd known—known with a spike of emotion that was like a punch to his guts—that he would never allow Ian or any other man to take Marisa from him. That whatever it cost he would take her back. However impossible, he would smash those problems to pieces and get what with every cell in his body over this punishing absence had grown more and more and more impossible to deny.

So he had let instinct—hot, overpowering instinct—take over. Take him from his desk, his office, London, and into his car, pressing pedal to the metal and storming his way westwards.

And now he was here—and so was Marisa, so was everything he wanted. Everything he was going to have.

No one and nothing was going to stop him. Not any more...

'You're out of Ian's life now, and that was what I had to achieve.' He looked at her, said what he knew he had to say. 'I didn't like what I was doing, Marisa, but I had to do it. Family is everything—and I had to protect my sister from the threat you represented to her. You can have no share in Ian's life. But,' he went on, 'you've accepted that, and I'm relieved to hear it—drastic though my method was. I acknowledge that.'

He held up a hand again, as if to brush aside the means he'd adopted to part his brother in law from her, and continued, getting to the most important part of his communication. The essential part. The part he'd driven over two hundred miles to deliver.

'Now we're free—both of us. Free to do what I have wanted to do since the moment I left you in your flat on our return.'

He got to his feet, crossed towards her. The narrow space between them disappeared. He reached out his hand, sliding it around the nape of her neck. The tendrils of damp hair were like silk on his fingertips. The scent of her body was like incense. The flush in her cheeks like roses. Her parted mouth was like honey waiting to be tasted...claimed...*reclaimed*...

'This,' he said, and his eyes poured down into hers like a golden haze, so that she was dizzy, blinded. Triumph surged in him—triumph and sweet, sweet possession...

He lowered his mouth to hers and bliss consumed her. She had dreamt of his kisses, yearned for them, craved them like an addict—and now it was happening. Here, now...

Bliss, sweet golden bliss.

He was drawing away from her again, but his hands were cupping her head, his body close against hers, his eyes still pouring down into hers.

'I've missed you so much,' he said. His voice was a husk. 'I can't do without you. And now, with you severed from Ian, I've realised I don't have to! I am free to take you back—to have again what I had before.'

His mouth started to lower again.

But, as if wires had jerked every muscle in her body, she yanked away. Stumbled around the corner of the table, getting it between them. Her eyes were wide and staring.

'Are you mad?' Her voice would hardly work and she had to swallow to make any sound come out. 'Are you *mad?*' she said again, louder now. Stronger.

Her mind was reeling. Reeling the way her body was. Her senses were aflame. But now water had been poured on them—an icy, frozen douche that doused them utterly. Emotion was knifing through her—but not the one she had just experienced, the bliss of his kiss. This was the one that had been coursing its way from deep, deep underground. That broke through now in a terrifying roar in her head.

'You lied to me from beginning to end! You lied to me and manipulated me and played me like a total idiot. How can you *possibly* think I would just take up with you again? That I would meekly go back to you after what you did to me? I'd have to be certifiable to do that.' She took a shuddering breath. 'Get out! Get out of here! I've done what you wanted me to do—given up Ian. So you've got no right—no right at all!—to come here and *dare* to say what you have.'

If he was reeling from her onslaught he didn't show it.

'You're angry with me—it's understandable,' he began. 'But—'

'Get out!' Her hands clenched the edge of the table. 'I don't ever want to see you again. I don't want anything to do with you ever again.'

His expression changed. 'Liar,' he said. 'You can't deny. It's impossible for you—just as it is for me, Marisa—to deny the effect we have on each other. Don't you think I curse the fact that I had to deceive you the way I did? I wish to God you'd never had anything to do with my damn brother-in-law in the first place. I wish I'd met you in any other circumstances. Because the effect you have on me would have been the same.'

He paused, his expression changing yet again. The molten, liquid lambency was back in his eyes, and his body language was charged with a voltage she would have to be blind, insensible not to recognise...to respond to.

'I might have lied to you about why I inveigled an acquaintance with you, lied about what purpose I had—but nothing else was a lie.' His eyes were resting on her, pouring into her. 'I never lied to you with my body...'

Breath rasped in her lungs, and her nails dug into the wood of the table's edge.

'Go!' she got out. 'I just want you to go.' She couldn't cope with this—she just couldn't. Ever since she'd seen him get out of his car she had been mentally shaking. But this—what he was saying...proposing...

'Marisa—listen to me.'

His voice sounded urgent. She couldn't bear it. Couldn't bear him being here, saying such things to her—asking such things of her.

She took another shuddering breath, not letting him speak as she cut across him. 'No! There's nothing on this earth that would ever make me even consider even for a single second what you are saying to me! How could you even think I would? Just how *stupid* do you think I am? After what you've done to me—said to me.'

He shook his head. Hell, this was all going wrong—totally wrong. He had to claw back somehow—anyhow. He had driven here with the devil on his tail, furious that Ian had dared to seek her out again, consumed with anger at his brother-in-law, consumed even more by an emotion he knew he had to name—could no longer deny.

Jealousy. Raw, open jealousy. Of Ian.

He's not having her. Never again! She's mine—and I want her back.

That was the stark, strident message he'd had to face up to as the miles had been eaten up by his foot on the accelerator. He had to get to her so that Ian couldn't try and persuade her back to him.

So that *he* could persuade her back to *him*.

So that she wouldn't haunt his dreams any more, or torment his memory, so that she could finally be to him what he wanted her to be—not the woman he'd had to sever from his brother-in-law but the woman he wanted for himself.

'Do you think I *wanted* to do what I did?' he demanded. 'But it's done now—finished. Over.'

Her eyes iced. 'Yes, that's exactly what it is. Finished. Over. And I don't mean Ian—I mean you. So, like I said, go—just go.'

'You don't mean that.' His voice was flat, disbelieving. 'If you're waiting for me to apologise for doing what I did the way I did it, then I can't. You had no business getting involved with my brother-in-law, and nothing can change that.' Again his voice changed. 'But having now seen where you come from, seen the kind of background you have, I can understand the temptation to inveigle yourself into his life. Gain from him the affluence and comfort you certainly don't have here.'

He looked around disparagingly at the cramped, shabby kitchen.

'I can make allowances,' he said. 'Understand *why* you found Ian so tempting.' His gaze swept back to her. 'You don't have to live like this, Marisa. Let me take you away from it all. We were good together. We can have it again—honestly, this time, with no more secrets.'

His eyes were blazing, rich and lambent, his voice deep, accented, sending vibrations through her.

'I want you to go.' Her voice was controlled. Very controlled over an emotion so strong that it might burst from her like an eruption. 'I don't want you here. I don't want anything more to do with you. And for your information, I don't want you to "take me away from it all". This happens to be my home. It may be poor, but it is mine, and it is where I live, and where I will go on living now.' She took a ragged breath. 'It's where I belong,' she finished.

Because this *was* where she belonged. She knew that now. Not in Ian's softly luxurious, pampering cocoon, kept secret from the world. And not—a jagged knife-thrust went through—dear God, *not* helplessly captive in Athan Teodarkis's cruel web of lies and deceit that had killed anything that she might once have felt for him.

Stony-faced, insistent, she stood her ground. 'So I want you to go,' she said again

Before she cracked, broke down, gave in—gave in to the desperate longing in her to throw herself into his arms, to pretend that nothing had come between them, to pretend that he'd never deliberately set out to seduce her and then denounce her the way he had. To pretend that what she'd thought was true *was*—he had never set her up, deceived her, lied to her...

But he had, and nothing could undo that

He wasn't saying anything. He was just standing there, tall and dark and so heart-stoppingly handsome that she could feel the power of it radiating like a force field. His face was a mask.

She'd seen it like that before when he'd confronted her on their return from St Cecile. When he'd closed himself to her, shut and locked the door, thrown away the key.

'I see,' he said. His voice was terse. Clipped. 'Well, you've made yourself very clear. So, yes, I'll go.'

Yet for a moment—a moment that seemed to hang in the

air like a weight—he remained motionless. She stood frozen, behind the table that divided her from him—behind everything that divided her from him and always would.

Always.

Then, 'I wish you well, Marisa. It would be…ungenerous of me to do less,' he said. His voice had no emotion, no depth. Nothing. Nothing at all.

His face still blank, still closed, he turned and walked out of the room.

She couldn't move. Could only wait while she heard his footsteps in the narrow corridor to the front door, and then the creaking door open and close behind him. For a few moments longer she waited. Only the crackling of the logs in the range was audible. Then another sound penetrated. A car engine gunning. Louder, then fading.

Fading completely.

He had gone.

Marisa went on standing there, quite motionless. Her eyes started to blink. Slowly, and then faster, tears began to run down her cheeks.

Along the narrow lane Athan drove—dangerously, recklessly fast. He had to. Had to gain as much distance from her as possible. He had arrived here a bare hour ago, driven by a demon he could not shake off his back. By the fear that she had succumbed to Ian Randall's forbidden blandishments, his begging to resume their affair. A demon had bitten him with the venom of savage jealousy.

Now a different demon drove him. Worse, much worse, than the first.

He wanted her—and she would not come to him.

I've lost her.

The words fell into his head like stones. Stones he could not shift. Stones that sat there crushing his thoughts, his emotions, everything.

All around him, pressing on the glass of the car windows, was darkness.

Darkness outside him.

Inside him.

He drove on into the winter's night.

CHAPTER SIX

MARISA dug carefully with the trowel. The garden her mother had loved so much had become overgrown, and she was trying to clear away the weeds from the new shoots sprouting up all over the flowerbeds. Spring had finally arrived, and as she knelt she could feel the sun warm on her back. It seemed like a blessing.

She was in need of blessings. Working hard to count them. To keep them in the forefront of her mind. Keep buried in the depths of her mind all remembrances of Athan Teodarkis— buried deep, buried safe.

She was humming to herself intermittently—some tune she'd heard on the radio. She listened to the radio a lot these days. It was companionship. Comforting. The cottage was so isolated she could play the radio out here in the garden knowing no one would be disturbed by it.

A robin was hopping around at the back of the flowerbed, tilting its head sideways and eyeing her hopefully. A small worm coiled itself under a clod of earth and she kept it buried. Fond as she was of the robin, who was a cheery visitor to the garden, she didn't feel up to deliberately feeding it a worm who was only trying to have a quiet life.

The way she was.

A quiet life. That was all she wanted right now. One that,

like the tiny earthworm could be spent buried deeply and safely. Sheltered and out of the way.

Where she belonged.

It had been weeks since Athan had been and gone. Weeks and weeks. How many, precisely, she hadn't counted. Hadn't wanted to. The days drifted by, one after another, marked only by the burgeoning spring. That followed a calendar that had its own schedule. One day it was a clump of primroses, unfurling their pale blossoms, another day the catkins showering her with golden pollen. Another the first flush of green on the once bare branches of the trees.

It was all she wanted right now.

She kept herself almost entirely to herself. She had set up a grocery delivery service with a supermarket in a large market town, and it suited her not to have to go there in person. The weekly delivery was good enough. Sometimes the local farmer's tractor rumbled past the cottage, but when she heard it coming she made sure she was not visible. She wasn't being deliberately stand-offish. She just didn't want to see anyone. Anyone at all. Whether local or stranger.

It was as if she was hibernating. Tucking herself away. Shutting down. Trying not to think. Trying not to feel. Trying to keep busy in the garden. While she worked she could feel her mother's presence, approving of her for what she was doing. Glad her daughter was back here again, safe in the haven she had found for herself—her refuge from a world that had rejected her, a man who had not wanted her.

Marisa's face twisted. Athan had wanted *her*.

That was the bitter, poisoned irony of it. After what he'd done to her, he wanted her.

Did he really think I would just totally ignore what he'd done? Why he'd done it? Just act like it had never happened?

But he had—obviously. That was what he'd assumed— that he could just pick her up again, carry on with her again. Take her back to his bed again...

No! She mustn't think like that—they were dangerous thoughts. Bringing in their wake memories that were even more dangerous. Lethal.

She dug deeper with the trowel, wrestling with a long, tenacious dandelion tap root to extract the last fragment. It wasn't the kind of root you could leave in the soil—a new weed would sprout even from the tiniest portion, seeking the air and the sun, thrusting up to grow and flourish.

Thoughts about Athan were like that. So were memories. She must get every last fragment of them out lest they seek to flourish once again.

She paused in her work, lifting her eyes to the hedge that bordered the garden, to the slope behind that led up onto open moorland. She would go for a walk later—blow away the cobwebs. Blow away the dangerous thoughts and memories that tried to get out.

Questions went through her mind and she wished she could have an answer to them, but knew she could not. Questions she had never asked but wished now she had. Questions of her mother.

How long did it take you to get over my father? To get him out of your head, your mind, your heart? To be free of him— free of what he'd done to you?

And the question that was most fearful of all: *Did you ever get over him?*

That was what she feared the most. That the wound was too deep, the scarring too brutal.

Because the problem was that despite all she was doing not to think about him, absorbing herself in this world, so familiar and so utterly different from the places she had been with Athan, it wasn't working. That was what she was scared of.

How long will it take to get over him?

That was the question that fretted at her, tormented her. She wanted not to think about not thinking about him. She wanted not to have to make this continual effort to turn her mind to other things. To immerse herself in this place she knew so well, surrounded by nature, by the wild landscape of the moors, the quiet fields and hedgerows.

But it didn't seem to be working—that was the problem. Surely by now she should at the very least be starting to forget him, to get over him. Not wanting to think about him, remember him. Surely she ought to be able to use her head to control her heart?

She froze. With one part of her brain she watched the robin hop closer to her. Bright-eyed. Red-breasted.

Predatory.

But the rest of her brain didn't see him. Didn't see the garden or the sunshine on the bushes, or the hedge behind the flowerbed.

The words that had sounded unconsciously in her mind came again.

Surely she ought to be able to use her head to control her heart?

No! She hadn't meant that—she hadn't. Panic filled her, choking in her throat.

It's not my heart—it's nothing to do with my heart.

Because if it was...

Before her eyes, the robin pounced. His sharp, deadly beak indented into the damp earth and in a flash, triumphantly, he tugged out the worm she'd tried to hide from him. With a flurry of wings he was gone, his prey consumed.

It's not my heart. I don't love him. I don't love him!

'Global economy...fiscal policy...employment levels...infrastructure investment...'

Athan let the words drone over his head. He wasn't listening. He gave the appearance of it, though—anything else would have been rude. But the speaker at the conference—a top economist at a major bank—had been going on for what seemed like for ever. And Athan had heard it all before—

several times now. This was the third day of the conference, and he had been here right from the start.

It mopped up time, this conference, and that was the most important aspect of it.

Time that he would otherwise have spent brooding.

Obsessing.

Because that was what it was, he knew. He could look it in the face and know it for what it was. Know *why* it was what it was.

He'd lost her. Plain and simple.

Devastating.

How had it happened? How had he screwed it up so badly? But he knew why—just didn't like accepting it. He'd high-tailed it down to the back of beyond where she'd holed up in that rundown hovel, seething with a raw, angry jealousy that he'd disguised to himself as outrage because Ian was daring to try and hook up with her again, and he'd hit a stone wall. Her point-blank refusal to have anything more to do with him.

Frustration warred with self-castigation. Frustration usually won—frustration that what he wanted so badly he wasn't going to get—but every now and then self-castigation managed to force itself through.

Did you really imagine that, having been manipulated and deceived, she was going to open her arms to you again? Take up with you again just where you left off—or rather, just before where you left off, at the bit where you hadn't yet denounced her as your brother-in-law's marriage-wrecker?

Of course she wasn't going to tamely come right back to him. Of course she was going to throw him out on his ear…

His eyes flashed darkly as he berated himself yet again.

You never stood a chance of getting her back. Not after what you did to her.

Then his expression hardened. Yes, well, she had no call to feel herself ill-used. *She* was the one who'd welcomed the attentions of a man she knew was married. That was what he had to remember. Then another thought flickered uncomfortably across his consciousness—that cramped, dilapidated cottage she lived in, stark evidence of a penurious background that would have meant Ian's lavish attentions being so very tempting to her. No wonder a practised, suave philanderer like his brother-in-law had been able to impress her, lead her astray. She'd fallen head first for his superficial charms and turned a conveniently blind eye to the wedding ring he wore.

That was what he had to remember. That was what justified what he'd done to her.

But another emotion slashed across his consciousness, obliterating any others. What did it matter now whether he was or was not justified in what he'd done? The fact that he'd done it had destroyed his chances of getting her back—that was all. Marisa had sent him packing and that was that. She was gone. He'd lost her.

All that was left was frustration.

One more emotion. One he was trying hard not to admit to. Because in comparison even the most obsessive frustration was easier to endure.

We were good together—it worked. I don't know precisely why, or how, but it did. It was easy being with her—natural.

His mind went back to that idyllic fortnight in the Caribbean, remembering how his mind had plucked so troublingly at what he was doing, what he was going to have to do when they went back to London, when he could no longer shut his eyes to the purpose he'd set out with, when he'd have to set aside what they were enjoying now and destroy it all…

Well, I did destroy it—and I can hardly sit here and complain that I can't get her back, can I? I did what I did for my sister's sake, and now I have to accept the consequences.

It was stern talk, and he knew he had to hand it out to himself. But even as he did so, he could hear another voice, deep inside.

Saving your sister's marriage has lost you something you will never recover...never...

His eyes gazed out unseeing over the conference hall.

His face as bleak as a winter wind.

Marisa turned down the radio and cocked her ears. It was a car approaching, she could tell. She frowned. It wasn't the day for her grocery delivery, and very little traffic other than heavy farm vehicles ventured this far along the dead-end lane. Setting down her paint roller and clambering off the chair she'd been standing on to reach the parlour ceiling she was busy painting, she made her way to the front door. As she got there an envelope came through the letterbox. Opening the door, she saw the postman getting back into his van and reversing. She gave him a half wave of acknowledgement and picked up the envelope. Her frown deepened. She got very little post, but the handwriting was familiar. She felt a knot start in her stomach.

It was from Ian.

Slowly, she took the envelope into the kitchen and slit it open, drawing out a handwritten letter.

My dearest Marisa—I have something I simply must say to you...

The knot tightened in her stomach, but she made herself read on. When she reached the end she stared for a moment, blinking.

Should she really do what Ian was asking?

It took her all day and all of a sleepless night to find the answer, but in the morning she dug out her mobile and texted him. It was the first time she'd contacted him since she'd sent him away—over a month ago now. He texted back almost instantly, cock-a-hoop, telling her he'd made the arrangements and all she had to do was get herself to Plymouth railway station. He would meet her at Paddington that afternoon.

His buoyancy did not elicit a similar response in her. Foreboding filled her. Should she really go ahead with this? She looked about her. The little cottage looked a lot better now than it had when she'd first fled back here. She'd subjected the whole place to a spring clean, and was now working her way round the rooms, brightening them with fresh paint. Outside, the garden was in full spring glory—daffodils thronging the beds, primroses nestling near the sun-warmed earth, the foliage in verdant green leaf. There was birdsong in the air, which was sweet and mild with the eventual promise of summer to come.

Could she really face leaving this remote, tranquil haven, where she had finally started to find some peace after all the torment she had been through? Could she really face going back up to London, doing what Ian wanted of her?

Becoming part of his life again...

Deep reluctance warred with longing.

But he was so adamant that now was the time. That he was finally brave enough to do what he knew with every fibre of his being he had to do. Tell the truth about them.

He said as much to her when he sat down with her over a drink in a pub close to Paddington station, where he had taken her after meeting the train.

'I've got to do it, Marisa,' he said, his expression full. 'I've got to tell Eva. And you have to be there when I tell her, so that she will believe how much you mean to me.'

Anxiety and doubt filled her eyes. 'Ian, I'm just not sure...'

'Well, I *am* sure,' he told her. He took her hand, squeezing it fondly. 'I won't live this lie any longer. I've tried to—God knows I've tried. I tried while you were here in London and I hated it—keeping you a secret the way I did. And I tried when you went back to Devon and buried yourself there. But

I hated it still—and I will go on hating it, Marisa, until we stop keeping this a secret.'

He took a breath and went on. 'Things are different now. It's not just that I've missed you like the devil since you went away, but things have changed for me, too. You know I chucked in the job at Eva's brother's company? Well, I'm glad I did. I've got another job, and it's one I really want to make something of.'

His expression changed, and Marisa could see the enthusiasm in it, hear the vigour in his voice.

'I've been taken on as marketing director of a third world fairtrade company that wants to tackle the supermarkets. I'm really fired up by it—it's a great cause, and I feel I can use my talents to do something important.' He made a rueful face. 'It also frees me from any sense of obligation or gratitude towards Eva's brother. In the circumstances—' he eyed Marisa meaningfully '—that's pretty much essential.'

He squeezed her hand again.

'Finally I feel I'm in a position to open up about you—to come clean. And that's what I want to do tonight.' He took one last decisive breath. 'We've got to do it, Marisa. You and me—telling the world about us.' He got to his feet, drawing her with him. Smiling down at her. 'Let's go and do it,' he said.

Still filled with anxiety, Marisa went with him.

Absently, Athan fingered a wine glass set out on the table in one of the hotel's private dining rooms. Eva was talking to the butler, telling him she'd changed her mind about what desserts to have.

For himself, Athan couldn't have cared less what she'd chosen for that evening. He had no appetite—none at all. Certainly not for this travesty of a 'family celebration' that Eva had said she was organising at her favourite Park Lane hotel.

'It was Ian's idea,' she'd said happily. 'He wants to tell you all about his new job. He's so excited by it—and so am I. It's as if there's a huge weight off his shoulders.'

Glancing at the vintage champagne on ice, the perfect damask napery, the silver service and the huge display of hothouse flowers, and knowing just what dinner in a private dining room cost at a place like this, it was just as well, Athan thought sourly, Ian had private means of his own—and that his wife was backed by the Teodarkis coffers. His new salary would not be nearly as generous as his old one had been.

Well, it was all to the good, he supposed. Not only did Eva seem very happy about it, but a demanding new job—even if poorly paid—had the notable benefit that it would keep his wayward brother's nose to the grindstone, with no time for dalliance. Athan's face hardened. At least there had been no sign of Ian trying to take up with Marisa again—nor was there any sign of him attempting to line up a replacement for her either. With luck, his sister's marriage might really be on the level again—at least for the time being.

His eyes shadowed. Something good had come out of the unholy mess that was Marisa Milburne's impact on his life. He'd better hang on to that. Find cold comfort in it.

He glanced out of the window over the rain-wet street beyond. He hadn't been to England since his fruitless pursuit of Marisa to the derelict dump she lived in. Hadn't been able to face it. Work, conferences—anything at all had kept him away—and he'd been glad of it. Coming here to London, now, for this dinner party his sister had organised, had not been on his itinerary, but Eva had pressed him so he'd reluctantly given in.

He was trying to be happy for her. Hell, it was to ensure *her* happiness that he'd gone and got himself into the mess he was now in with Marisa—so of course he had to be glad for his sister. Whether her happiness would last, of course, was a completely different thing.

He gave a heavy sigh. Well, at least he'd achieved his original purpose. He'd have to be content with that. Now he just had to get through this evening's dinner party, say whatever was appropriate in the circumstances by way of congratulating Ian on getting a new job, standing on his own feet, not cheating on his wife any more—not that he could mention that last, of course. At least not in front of Eva.

'Athan?' Eva had finished with the butler. 'I'm just going to go and check my make up in the powder room. Ian should be here any moment.'

She wafted by and Athan nodded at the butler, dismissing him for the moment. He wanted to be alone, even for a brief while. To steel himself for the ordeal ahead. Could he really get through an entire meal with Ian, knowing that he knew about the infidelity he'd planned, with both of them putting on a good front for Eva?

Well, he'd have to try—damn hard!—that was all.

The doors to the private dining room opened, and Athan turned back from gazing bleakly out of the window.

As he turned, he froze.

Ian had just walked in.

In his wake, stepping with obvious trepidation, was Marisa.

Athan's reaction was instant. 'You *dare* to bring her here!' he hurled at his brother-in-law.

Marisa could feel the breath congeal in her lungs. How could this be happening? She felt faint, clinging automatically to Ian's arm as if to keep herself upright. Oh, dear God, if she'd had the faintest idea Athan would be here...

Ian had stiffened. 'Where's Eva?' he demanded.

Athan ignored the question. His expression was a mask of fury. 'You have *one* second to get that woman out of here before—'

'Before what?' A light, feminine voice sounded from the doorway.

Athan whirled round. His sister stood poised in the doorway, looking at the tableau frozen in front of her. Her expression changed when her gaze took in the presence of a completely strange woman on her husband's arm.

'Ian?' she said enquiringly, a bemused but unsuspicious look on her face.

Marisa swallowed. So, finally, this was Ian's wife. She could feel her thoughts racing in her head, tried to get control of her emotions. Emotions that had been erratic enough ever since she'd read Ian's letter that morning. But when she'd felt the full force of her dismay at Athan's presence here she'd reeled.

Oh, God, she couldn't do this! She had to get out of here—now. Jerkily, she stumbled forward, heading for the door, and Eva automatically stepped aside. Her expression was changing from bemusement to astonishment. Marisa threw her an agonised look.

'I'm sorry. So sorry—I can't do this! I—'

Suddenly her arm was taken. A deep, harsh voice spoke—but not to her.

'Eva—I'll deal with this.'

Athan's hand around her forearm was like a steel clamp, hustling her out. Out of his sister's presence—before her worthless snake of a husband could inflict the blow he was so obviously, outrageously intending to. Rage consumed him.

What the hell is he thinking of—to bring Marisa here? To confront Eva with her?

It could mean only one thing—the very worst. Ian was going to tell Eva he was leaving her…

But not for Marisa Milburne—not for her!

Emotions seared within him—utterly disparate, but inextricably entwined. To protect his sister from her cheating rat of a husband—to stop Marisa going off with anyone, anyone at all.

Except himself.

Possessiveness scalded within him. Just seeing her there,

despite his anger at realising what Ian was intending, had been like a shockwave through his senses.

He thrust her out into the wide, deserted corridor beyond, yanking the dining room door shut behind him and dragging her down towards the elevator. His only thought was to get her out of the hotel—away from Eva. But was Ian already spilling his treacherous guts to her? Hell and damnation—he could slug him to kingdom come for this!

He jabbed furiously at the elevator button and rounded on Marisa.

'You despicable little bitch! How dare you? How dare you walk in, bold as brass, with Ian?'

Marisa paled, trying to drag herself away from him, but it was impossible. His hand was like steel around her arm.

'I'm sorry! I knew I shouldn't have gone along with Ian.'

Athan shook her like a rag, his face black. 'Then why the hell *did* you?'

'Because we've had enough of this endless secrecy!' she cried. 'He convinced me we couldn't hide it any longer. He refuses to hide me away any more. I won't be his sordid little secret.'

He dropped her arm. It fell to her side limply. She swallowed, just looking at him. His face was like granite. Emotion scythed through her.

'But whether Eva knows about you or not, you *are* the "sordid little secret", aren't you?' he said, his voice low and knifing. 'And telling her won't make you any less sordid.'

She shut her eyes. 'I know,' she said heavily. 'And I know that walking out now isn't going to mend anything. She'll be wondering who I am, why Ian brought me here tonight. So even if I walk out now it's too late—'

He swore in his own language, the Greek words harsh. 'Then there is only one thing to be done—only one way to hide it from her.'

She looked at him. He took her arm again. His mind

was working frantically, trying to work out how to salvage something from this unholy mess. This was a denouement he hadn't foreseen.

I thought Ian had let her go—and all along he was planning this.

Rage consumed him. Rage at Ian—and rage at himself for not realising what a treacherous little rat the man truly was.

He took a heavy breath, marshalled his thoughts.

'I'll tell Eva you're here on my account. That Ian was escorting you to the hotel for me as I've only just arrived from Athens. That I wanted to introduce you to her.' He finished heavily, his words biting and accusing, 'That way I might just manage to protect her from the sordid truth of your existence. After all—' his lip curled '—better that you are *my* mistress than her husband's.'

He made to steer her back towards the dining room..

But she wouldn't move.

She was looking at him. Staring at him. Just staring.

There was no emotion in her face. None whatsoever. Then slowly, very slowly, she peeled his fingers off her arm, and stepped away. He looked down at her, frowning. What the hell was she playing at now?

'Athan! Come back in!'

He slewed round sharply. Eva was in the dining room doorway, beckoning to him. Ian was standing beside her. Athan's head whipped back. Marisa had started to walk forward, towards the couple. There was purpose in her steps.

As they all went back inside the dining room and he closed the door on the four of them a sense of doom came over Athan. It was going to happen. The ugly, painful disclosure of the 'sordid little secret' that he'd gone to so much trouble to keep hidden from his sister. And all for nothing. For this—for his sister to be humiliated and her heart broken. Well, at least he would be there for her. Ready to let her sob on his shoulder after her husband had walked out on her with his mistress on his arm.

His mouth twisted, but there was no humour in it.

The mistress I want for myself...

But that wasn't going to happen. All that was going to happen was the destruction of his sister's fragile marriage. Well, better it ended now than later. Better never to love than to have love smashed to pieces...

He should know...

A blade like a vicious shard of ice slid into his side. He watched Marisa walk up to his sister. Watched Ian smile at her reassuringly.

Intimately.

Watched his sister frown wonderingly.

He went to stand beside her, opposite her husband. Opposite the woman who was never going to be anything more to do with him—who was going to take his sister's husband from her.

He should have felt rage. Fury. Black murderous anger for his sister's sake. For his own. But all there was inside him was an empty, bleak hollow. His eyes went to Marisa. She was looking so pale. So pale and so incredibly beautiful. She was standing beside Ian. They made a startlingly handsome couple—both so blond and blue-eyed, with their English complexions. A matched pair—a foil for his and his sister's dark, Mediterranean looks.

The blade slid into his guts, twisting its sharp, serrated edge as he gazed at Marisa.

Not mine. Never mine. Never—

'Eva—'

Ian's voice jolted him. It was thin, but resolute. Athan stood beside his sister, waiting for the axe to fall so he could pick up the pieces when it did. His face was still, like granite. Marisa's had no expression in it at all.

She would not meet his eyes. Well, that was understandable...

'Eva—' Ian said his wife's name again—stronger this time. He squared his shoulders. 'I've got something I have to say to you,' he said.

The puzzled look on Eva's face deepened.

'I've got to tell you something you will not like, that will be upsetting, but it has to be said. I asked Marisa here tonight for a particular reason. To tell you about her.'

Athan could keep silent no longer. He started forward, placing his hand on his sister's wrist, intending to speak Greek to her. He had to tell her himself—he could not let her bastard of a husband proclaim it.

'No!'

Marisa's sudden interjection silenced him before he had even started. His head swivelled to her. For a moment he reeled. The expression blazing from her eyes was like a hundred lasers.

'Ian will tell her,' she bit out. Her face snapped round to the man at her side. 'Go on! Tell her. Tell *him*.'

There was something wrong with her voice, Athan registered. She had never spoken like that before. Even when she'd been ordering him from that tumbledown cottage of hers. This was like ice—ice made from the coldest water.

Ian's expression flickered, as if he was taken aback by her tone. Then he looked straight at his wife again.

'There is no easy way to tell you this,' he said. 'So I'm just going to say it straight out. Marisa—' he said, and as he spoke he reached for her hand.

She let him take it, curled her fingers around it, warm and familiar, stepping forward slightly, aligning herself with him. A couple. Together.

Like a guillotine cutting down, Athan spoke. Contempt was in his voice, harsh and killing.

'Marisa is his mis—'

'—is my sister.'

The words fell like stones from a great height, crushing Athan dead.

Marisa looked at Athan, her face still completely, totally expressionless.

'I'm Ian's sister,' she said.

CHAPTER SEVEN

Had the world stopped moving? It must have, thought Athan with what was still working in his brain, because everything else seemed to have stopped. Including his breathing. Then, explosively, it restarted.

'His *sister?*' Shock reverberated in his voice.

Marisa's gaze was levelled at him, still expressionless. Like a basilisk's gaze.

She might have laughed to see the shock on his face—but she wasn't in the mood for laughing. She was in the mood for killing.

Anger—dark, murderous anger—was leashing itself tighter and tighter around her. She had to hold it down—hold it tight down. Because it if escaped...

'Ian's *sister?*' The voice this time was Eva's, and all it held in it was complete bewilderment. 'But Ian hasn't got a sister.'

Marisa's eyes went to Ian, knowing that this was the moment they had dreaded but now had to face. She saw him draw breath, then open his mouth to speak.

'I didn't know—I didn't know about Marisa. Not until very recently.' He took another breath. 'Look, maybe we should all sit down. It's...it's complicated, and it's going to be... difficult,' he said.

He gestured towards the table and after a moment's hesitation Eva went and took her place.

Marisa did likewise. Her body felt very stiff. Immobile. She watched Athan stalk to the other side and sit himself down opposite her, while Ian took his place opposite his wife. Just like two couples settling down to a dinner party. As though a bombshell hadn't just exploded in the middle of them.

'I don't know about you, but I could do with a glass of wine,' Ian said in a shaky voice, trying, Marisa knew, to keep it light.

He reached for the bottle of white wine cooling in its chiller, and for the next few moments there was a hiatus while he poured four glasses and handed them round. Instinctively Marisa found herself taking a gulp.

She needed it.

As she set the glass back on the pristine white tablecloth she realised her hand was trembling slightly. Involuntarily, her eyes glanced across at the dark figure sitting opposite her. His face was like marble—showing absolutely nothing.

Emotion spiked in her, but she crushed it down. She mustn't let anything out—nothing at all. She was here to support Ian, that was all. And he, poor lamb, looked drawn. She watched him take a generous mouthful of wine, then he straightened his shoulders, looked straight across at his wife, and started.

'Marisa is my half-sister,' he said. 'We share the same father. But Marisa's mother—' He stopped.

Across the table, Marisa could see Athan tense. Her eyes went to his. For one brief moment they met, and in them she could see that he knew exactly what was going to be said next.

And it would have to be by her. It wasn't fair to get Ian to say it.

'My mother...' She swallowed, turning her gaze to include Eva. 'My mother was Ian's father's mistress.'

She dropped her gaze, unable to continue for a moment. Emotion welled in her like a huge, stifling balloon.

Eva said something. It was in Greek. Even to Marisa's untrained ears it sounded shocked.

But she dimly realised it didn't sound surprised...

Ian was talking again, and she could hear in his voice what she had heard before so often when they had talked about themselves and their backgrounds: a weary resignation.

'You both know what he was like—Eva, you of all people know because of your mother's long friendship with mine—how she supported my mother through so many unhappy years. Even when my father threatened your parents' marriage with his troublemaking.' He took another mouthful of wine, as though he still needed it. 'Marisa's mother wasn't the first of his mistresses and she certainly wasn't the last. But she was...' He paused, and now he reached his hand out and slipped it comfortingly around Marisa's wrist. 'She was the only one who made the terrible mistake of falling in love with him.'

Marisa spoke. Her voice was low, and she couldn't look at Eva—let alone Athan. Above all not Athan.

'I don't exonerate her. She knew he was married. But she told me that he always said it was a marriage wherein both partners understood—' her voice twisted '—understood that it was primarily about business and property, preserving wealth and inheritance and so on, and that he had never married for love.' Marisa took another breath, lifting her eyes this time and they were filled with a bleak, sad pity for her foolish, trusting, self-blinded mother. 'She chose to believe him. He pursued her relentlessly because she'd said no to him.' Her voice twisted again. 'He wasn't a man who liked women to say no to him, so he told her whatever he considered effective in getting her into bed. He told her his wife had met someone else and asked for a divorce.' Her voice became tight. 'When she had yielded to him, and subsequently found herself pregnant, he suddenly didn't want to know any more. And she realised far too late how stupid she had been.'

She took a heavy breath.

'He gave her a lump sum—enough to buy the cottage I was brought up in—and a small income to go with it. He got her to sign a document waiving all claims to official child support from him. She was too devastated to refuse, and she went along with being bundled out of his life and kept quiet. She moved to Devon and disappeared. I grew up having no idea who he was—only that he was "the great love of her life," as she used to say. After she died I came to London to try and find him. But I had no name and nothing to go on but a photograph my mother had kept—'

'Which is how she found me,' Ian interjected. 'It was total, absolute chance. Marisa took a job at a cleaning company and my office was one of their contracts. One evening I was working late. She saw me, stared at me—and that's how we found each other.'

'Of *course*,' Eva said slowly, comprehension dawning. 'Ian looks the image of his father…and presumably the photo was of a man around his age?'

Marisa nodded. She could say no more.

'It's extraordinary,' Eva breathed. 'To have absolutely no idea that you had a sibling.' She turned to her brother. 'Athan, imagine not knowing you even existed—it would be dreadful.'

He didn't respond. Then, abruptly, he got to his feet.

'Excuse me. I must—'

He stopped. There was nothing he 'must' do except get out of there.

'Athan?'

Eva's voice was bewildered, but he couldn't help it. He couldn't help anything right now. He just had to walk out.

Without another word he left the room, ignoring Eva's astonished rush of Greek at him, asking what on earth he was doing. Like an automaton he strode to the bank of lifts, jabbing at the button, willing the doors to open and let him escape. Leave. Get away. Away from her.

Away from what he'd done to her...

Inside the private dining room Eva was still staring, nonplussed, at her brother's empty place.

'What on earth—?' she began.

Her bewildered gaze came back to her husband, then moved on to Marisa. She started to speak, but Marisa spoke instead.

'I'm sorry—I have to—' Her voice was staccato and she couldn't finish. All she could do was get to her feet, roughly pushing back her chair, seize up her clutch bag and leave the room.

She could hear her half-brother call her name anxiously, but she ignored it.

Outside, the hotel corridor was deserted.

All except for the tall, dark figure standing by the elevator.

Sudden slicing memory knifed through her. Herself emerging from the elevator on her way back to the apartment Ian had leased for her, seeing the tall, dark figure striding towards her, asking her to keep the doors open for her.

A set up. That was all it had been. A calculating, carefully timed set-up with one purpose only.

To snare her. Captivate her.

Seduce her.

Seduce her away from the man he'd assumed she was having an affair with. A married man. His own brother-in-law.

Emotion buckled through her—hot and nauseating. Icy and punishing.

'Wait!'

Her voice carried the length of the deserted corridor, made him turn instantly. His expression froze. She strode up to him. The anger she'd kept leashed so tightly inside her while she'd sat at the table and told of her relationship with Ian, leapt in her throat. She stopped dead in front of him. Of its own volition her hand lifted, and she brought it across his face in a ringing slap.

'*That's* for what you thought I was!'

Then, in a whirl of skirts, she pushed past him into the lift that was opening its doors behind him, jabbed the 'close' button urgently.

But he made no attempt to follow her—made no movement at all. Only turned very slowly and watched her as the doors closed and the elevator swept her up to the bedroom floors. Her heart was pounding. In her vision seared the image of his face. Like a dead man's, with a weal forming across his cheekbone. Livid and ugly.

Marisa was walking. She did a lot of walking these days. Miles and miles. All over the moor. But however far she walked she never got away from what was eating her. Consuming her.

Destroying her.

Round and round the destructive thoughts went in her head. Over and over again she tumbled them.

How could she not have realised what it was that Athan thought about her? How could it not have penetrated through her thick, stupid skull that he had jumped to the conclusion about her that he had?

With hindsight—that most pointless and excruciating of all things—it was glaringly, blazingly obvious that that was what he had assumed all along

She'd replayed every line of that conversation—their ugly, utterly misbegotten conversation—where she had completely failed to understand just what he'd meant about her relationship with Ian.

I assumed he meant he'd discovered I was his sister. I never dreamt he thought anything so sleazy about me—anything so vile.

But that was exactly what he had done.

Right from the start.

She wanted to scream and yell and denounce him to the world. But there was no one she could tell. All she could do was swallow it down herself and keep it down. Keep totally out of everyone's way. Bury herself down her in Devon again—for ever this time.

The way she should have done first time around.

I should never have let Ian persuade me to go up to London to tell Eva about me. Because of what Athan did—because I can't tell Ian what he did—I can't have anything to do with him and Eva anyway. I can't ever look at Athan again—I can't bear to!

Emotion seared in her, hot and scalding.

How can I ever have anything more to do with a man like that? A man I hate with every fibre of my being.

Because of course she hated him. What else was it possible to feel about Athan Teodarkis now? Nothing. Only hatred. Black and venomous.

All consuming.

All destroying.

She trudged on. The rising slope had peaked, and now she was on the low crest looking down onto the half-buried remains of the Bronze Age village below the tor. Someone was standing in the middle of the site, which wasn't fenced off—there was very little damage walkers could do to such meagre remains.

At first when saw the solitary figure from the distance she was at she took no notice. On a warm day like this, in full Dartmoor spring, fellow walkers and ramblers on the moor were commonplace. But as she headed along the path that would take her past the site she stilled. There was something very familiar about the motionless figure.

He was looking towards her. Hands in his jacket pockets, legs slightly apart. The wind was ruffling his hair. His eyes were slightly narrowed against the sun behind her.

In a kind of daze—a mental suspension that kept one foot moving after another—she carried on down the slope towards the ancient village where once a whole community had thrived—living, loving, dying...

Now not even their ghosts remained to haunt the sunlit, windswept air.

He moved towards her, intersecting her path. Waiting for her.

She came up to him. Said nothing. Did nothing. Only stood there, her hands plunged into her anorak pockets, her face a mask.

Like his.

'Ian told me you were back here.' His voice was terse. Low. Strained.

'I gave you time,' he said. 'I gave us both time. But now we have to talk.'

She looked at him. Just looked at him. 'There is absolutely nothing to say,' she stated.

She was calm. Very calm. Amazingly calm, considering the seething tumult that had been inside her only moments ago, racking through her with all the unbearable impossibilities of the situation, the destructive morass of it all.

'You know that's not true,' he contradicted her.

Something flared in her eyes, then died again. Quenched.

'Well, what *is* there to say, then?' she threw at him, hands digging deeper into her pockets.

This was unreal—unreal to be standing here, beside a place where people had once lived and loved and died, nothing more than shards of bone in the earth now, who could feel no pain or loss any more, no emotions—nothing. Unreal to be standing in such a place and confronting the man who had driven her back here.

'What is there to say?' she demanded again. She stared at him, unblinking. Unflinching. 'You thought I was Ian's mistress, so you seduced me to take my mind off him while he went back to his wife—your sister. Now you've discovered that actually I wasn't his mistress after all. I'm his sister. And because I can't stomach having any more contact with *you,* it means I can't have anything to do with Ian or Eva, so telling Eva about me actually turns out to be have been a totally pointless exercise all round! There.' She took a sharp, incising breath, glaring at him. 'Does that just about sum up why there isn't the slightest thing more to be said on the subject?'

Expressions worked in his face and his jaw tightened. 'No, it doesn't.' He gave a heavy sigh. 'You know it doesn't. It doesn't even begin to get to the reason why we have to talk.'

He took her arm. She tried to shake it off, but he simply led her to a nearby lichen-covered drystone wall and sat her down on it, lowering himself beside her. She edged away and she knew he could see she'd done it, and she was coldly, savagely pleased. She was still calm—still amazingly, icily calm. It was like being inside an iceberg, and it suited her fine—just fine. She waited for him to drop his grip on her, but he didn't. She wouldn't flatter him by shaking herself free. She would just endure that tight, hard clasp. It would remind her of how much she hated him.

He turned to look at her. She closed her face. She wanted to close her eyes, but again that would have shown him that she was affected by him. And she wasn't affected—not at all.

She never would be. Never again.

He spoke abruptly. 'This is what I don't understand. That you didn't realise I'd thought Ian had set you up as his mistress. Surely to God you must have done?' His face worked. 'Why the hell else would I have done what I did—said what I said? Why else would I have done or said those things to you? Just because you were Ian's *sister?* Why the *hell* did you and Ian hide your relationship from everyone?'

Marisa's eyes widened. 'How can you even ask that? You know how close Eva is to Ian's mother—her godmother. How she's become like a second mother to her, taking her own mother's place. That's why we were so reluctant to tell Eva. Because it would have torn her loyalties in two. How could she have anything to do with her husband's sister when that sister was living proof of just how much Sheila Randall was hurt and betrayed by her husband?'

She swallowed. 'After I fled London, telling Ian it was because I couldn't go on hiding in the shadows, and he got a new job without your patronage, he became determined not to go on concealing such an important part of his life from his wife. It was a new start for him, and however difficult it was going to be he didn't want any secrets from Eva any more. Even the secret of my existence,' she finished bitterly.

Athan was silent a moment. Then he spoke. His voice was heavy—as heavy as the lead that seemed to be weighing him down, crushing him.

'I thought Ian was like his father. Incapable of fidelity. I've always thought it—feared it. I never approved of his marriage to Eva. Thought him lightweight. Superficial. Unworthy of my sister. And I thought that she was doomed to follow the same path as her mother-in-law, whose life was made a misery by her faithless husband.'

He paused, glancing briefly at Marisa and then away again, because it hurt too much to do otherwise. 'When my suspicions became aroused I took out surveillance on him. I found out about your existence—that you were living in an apartment he was paying for. There was no doubt about it. There were photos of you and him in a restaurant. Intimate photos that showed you and he billing and cooing over each other.' He paused again. 'And one of the photographs showed Ian giving you a diamond necklace.' Another pause, briefer this time, then words broke from him—harsh and hard. 'What the *hell* was I supposed to think? My brother-in-law was giving another woman a diamond necklace!'

Marisa stiffened.

'It was Ian's grandmother's. Our father's mother's necklace. He wanted me to have it. He wanted me to have all the things that our father had denied me—wanted to lift me out of the poverty that my father had condemned my mother to.' She looked away—far away—back into the past to her childhood. 'She knew she should never have given in to my father. Knew she was at fault. Knew she was a fool to love him. Knew she deserved what she got from him—rejection and short shrift. It was a lesson, she taught me well,' she said heavily. Her eyes came back to Athan. 'Which is why it was so unbearable to realise you thought I'd stoop to carrying on with a married man. Why I was so angry that evening Ian told Eva about me.'

Athan's face was drawn. 'You had every right to be.' His voice was sombre. 'I misjudged you totally. Thought the very worst of you.'

She could hear the self-laceration in his voice, and something twisted inside her.

'I hated you for it!' she burst out. 'I thought I hated you for what you did to me—deliberately seducing me. But when I realised…realised that what you thought of me was a million times worse than simply trying to latch on to my wealthy brother and mess up his family…oh, then I hated you a million times more than I did before.' She felt her hands fist in her pockets. 'When I threw in your face what I truly was to Ian—what our relationship actually is—oh, it felt so damn *good*. Wiping that condemning contempt off your face. And slapping you felt even *better*!'

She jerked to her feet, yanking her arm free of him. Standing there, buckling with emotion, she swayed in the wind, her face convulsed.

Why had he come here? To torment her again? What *for*?

It was over now—all over. Nothing more to be done, or said. It was all a mess—a hideous, insoluble mess. But she knew she had to accept that in the end, it wasn't his fault.

Heavily, she turned around to face him again. He hadn't moved. Was just sitting there immobile, looking at her.

His expression was…

Was what? she thought, finding thoughts skittering across her mind inchoately, incoherently.

Wary—that was what it was. But there was more than wariness in it. His eyes—his dark, gold-flecked eyes, whose glance had once turned her to jelly—were now regarding her with…

Such bleakness.

That was what was in his face. His eyes.

She took a scissoring breath. 'There isn't any point to this—there really isn't. It's just a mess—a total mess all round. I can see…understand…why you jumped to the conclusion you did. I can see why you wanted to protect your sister. You did what you thought best at the time. But now… now that it's all out in the open—the actual truth, not your assumption—it just makes it impossible for me to have anything more to do with you, or Eva—or even Ian, really. I can't ever see you again—you must see that. What you did to me will always be there, poisoning everything.' She looked at him. Looked into those dark, wary, bleak eyes. 'I can't get over what you did—I will never be able to get over what you did.'

For one long, unbearable moment they just gazed at each other across everything that divided them. An impossible divide.

A huge, crushing weariness pressed down on her. Her head bowed. She knew she should head for home, back to the sanctuary of her cottage. But her legs were suddenly like lead.

Then behind her she heard a movement. Hands lightly—so lightly—touched her hunched shoulders, then dropped away.

'And nor will I.'

Athan's voice was low. Conflict filled it. Filled his head. Was she right? Should he never have come here? Never have followed the crushing imperative to find her—talk to her? Because he *had* to talk to her. He couldn't just leave it the way it had been—with her denouncing, punishing slap ringing across his mind. His soul.

Punishing him for what he had thought about her. Punishing him for what he'd done to her. Punishing him for getting her totally, utterly wrong...

'It will be like a brand on me all my life,' he told her. 'What I did to you.'

She gave a little shrug. It was all she could manage. 'It doesn't matter. I understand why you did it. It was a... misunderstanding, that's all.' Her voice gave a little choke as she said the word that was so hideous an understatement. 'A mess up. But it doesn't matter. In the end it doesn't leave any of us worse off, does it? If anything, Ian and Eva's marriage is stronger than ever, so that's surely some good out of it. He finally has a job where he feels he can not only make a real contribution to the world, in a way he never could before, but he can stand on his own two feet—out from under your shadow. Plus, of course—' her voice twisted '—he has finally won your trust—convinced you he's not cut from the same corrupt cloth as our father. So that's all to the good, isn't it?'

She spoke negligently, carelessly. As if nothing mattered any more—just as she was saying.

'As for you and me—' She swallowed. There was a stone in her throat. Making it hard to speak. Impossible almost. But she had to force the words all the same.

She stared out ahead of her, towards the granite tor beyond. Rocks that had thrust up out of the burning earth so deep below, then cooled and congealed in the air. Hardened and set. Unchangeable now. Only the wind and the rain would weather them, wear them down over aeons of time. Aeons that mocked the brief, agonised flurry of human lives. Just as the vanished ghosts of the dead village they stood in haunted those who came after them.

'As for you and me,' she said again, 'what does it matter? What happened was…a mistake. An error. Regrettable, but understandable. It can't be mended, but—' The stone was harder now in her throat, but she had to get the words past it all the same. 'It can be ignored.'

She heard his intake of breath behind her. Then, carefully, he spoke.

'No—it can't. It can't be ignored. It has to be faced. I have to face it.'

The hands came again—lightly, briefly, on her shoulders. She could barely feel them, yet it was like electricity shivering within her as he turned her around to face him. Face what he was going to say.

His expression was sombre. The bleakness in his eyes was absolute.

'I wronged you. I wronged you and I will regret that all my life—however unintentioned it was, the wrong remains. But if you ask me to regret what happened, then…I won't. I can't. I came here to you afterwards wanting only one thing. Thinking that because you were now no longer a danger to my sister I could indulge myself—take from you what I wanted so, so badly. Have you back for myself again.'

He gazed down at her, and behind the bleakness in his eyes something else flared. Something that was dangerous to her. That threatened her. That sought to set aside the aeons of time that formed the moors, the millennia that separated them from the people who had once dwelt here in the shadow of the tors. That sought to mock the effect of time on human lives.

Something that was stronger than time. That would outlast all things.

'To have you back,' he said. 'To have you as you were in that brief, precious time we had—a time that enraptured me. And tormented me. Tormented me because I knew it was only a fleeting bubble—a bubble I would have to burst, cruelly and callously, when I denounced you.'

Emotion came to his eyes again, but it was stormy now. 'I hated what I had to do—hated what I thought you were. It made me even harsher to you than I had to be. And when I followed you down here, saw how you lived, I could see how Ian must have turned your head, beguiled you…led you astray.' He paused again, then said what needed to be said. 'Just as his father led your mother astray.'

Her eyes fell. She could not answer him. He answered for her.

'We're human, all of us, Marisa. We make mistakes. Your mother made hers. I made mine—misjudging you. Misjudging Ian.'

He paused and her gaze flickered back up to him. The bleakness was back in his eyes.

'We make mistakes and then we pay for them. Your mother paid for hers. I shall pay for mine.' He paused. 'Mine…my payment…will be doing without you.' He took a razored breath. 'I won't impose upon you by giving a name to why that will exact a price from me, but be assured it will be a heavier price than I ever imagined possible.' His mouth twisted. 'A price I didn't know existed until I started paying it.'

He lifted a hand as if to bid her farewell, as if to bid farewell to many things.

'I'll go now,' he said. 'I wish you well—it's all I can do, isn't it? All that you could possibly want me to do. I wish you well and leave you be.' He looked around him, across the wide, sunlit moorland, ablaze now with gorse and new growth, at the blue sky above arcing from east to west. A wild bird was singing somewhere as it rose on currents of air. Then his eyes came back to her.

Looked their last on her.

He felt the knife slide into his heart as he tore his gaze away again, and set it instead on the lofty tor beyond, piercing the sky with its dark, impenetrable mass. He started to walk towards it, following the path that led there, leaving her behind.

She watched him go. Watched his figure start to recede. Watched him walk out of her life.

There was a haze over the sun. Which was strange, because there were no clouds in the cerulean sky. Yet the haze was there, like a mist in her vision. She blinked, but it did not clear.

Only the wind stung her eyes, beading her lashes with a misty haze.

Thoughts crowded into her head. She could make no sense of them. They jumbled and jostled and each one cried for space. Then one—only one—stilled the others. Formed itself into words inside her head. She heard them, made herself hear them, even as she stood there, watching him walk away from her...

The words came again in her head. Athan's words.

'We make mistakes. Your mother made hers. I made mine...'

They came again, circling like a plane. Bringing more words in their wake.

What if I'm making my mistake now?

Her mother had ruined her life, giving her love to a man—a man who had proved utterly unworthy, totally deceitful and uncaring—instead of telling him to leave her alone, get out of her life before he could destroy it.

But what if my mistake is the opposite one?

The thought hung blazing in her mind.

What if my mistake is to let go of a man I should never let go? A man I should clutch to me and hold tight in my arms?

A man it would be—will be—an agony to lose?

Her eyes held to the figure striding away from her, getting further and further away. The air in her lungs seemed to turn to granite. Impossible to breathe. Impossible.

'Wait!' The word tore from her, freeing her breath. 'Athan! *Wait!*'

He stopped. Stopped dead. Froze. Then, as she stood, heart hammering in her chest, he turned.

She didn't speak, didn't cry out again. She had no thoughts, or words, or breath. She started forward, stumbling at first over the uneven ground, then found her balance, running now, faster and yet faster. The wind whipped the haze to her eyes, blinding her, but it didn't matter. She knew where she was going. Knew it with every fibre of her being. Knew the only place she would ever want to be.

He caught her as she reached him. Caught her in an embrace that swept her off the ground, swept her round and round as his arms wrapped her to him. She was crying, sobbing, but it didn't matter—nothing mattered. Nothing at all would ever matter—only this...this.

Being in his arms.

Loving him.

Loving him so, so much!

He was saying her name. Over and over again. Kissing her hair, clutching her to him. She was crying, and then she was laughing, and he was lowering her down so she could feel the ground beneath her feet again, but her arms were still wrapped around him so tightly, so close she would never let him go—*never* let him go....

'Oh, my darling—my darling one!'

Was that her speaking or him? It didn't matter—nothing mattered but this. The joy surging through her, the love...

Then he was loosening his arms around her, cupping her upturned face with his hands, his eyes blazing down into hers.

All bleakness was gone.

Only love—blazing.

And slowly, beneath the towering tor, which had no power to mock what stood so far beyond the power of time, circled by the ghosts of those who had lived and loved here so long ago, he lowered his mouth to hers and kissed her.

'This is love,' he said. 'This is my love for you. For all that

I did to you, this is why I cannot regret it. Because it gave you to me.' He took a painful breath, his eyes full. 'I didn't realise what it was…what was happening to me…until I lost you. Lost you, my dearest one, over and over again. So many times. I lost you when I said those cruel, denouncing words to you. Lost you when, eaten by jealousy of Ian, I chased you down here. I wanted to grab you back like a spoilt child deprived of what he wanted. I lost you when you threw the truth about yourself in my face at that nightmare dinner. Lost you when you walked up to me and vented all your anger for what I'd thought about you. Lost you over and over and over again.' His hands cupping her face pressed more urgently. 'And with each loss it hammered home to me more what was happening. That I was falling in love with you.'

He shuddered, and she felt his pain and clung to him more closely.

'Falling in love with you…even as I was losing you…over and over again…'

She gave a little cry, kissed him again to obliterate the pain she saw in him.

'I feared loving you,' she said 'Feared it so much. When I saw you sometimes on St Cecile, looking at me when you thought I couldn't see you, you looked so…so remote. I thought it was because you knew I was falling for you when you only wanted something passing that would end when we returned. That's what I thought when you said you needed to speak to me. I was steeled for it—ready for you to tell me it was over. I had the strength to bear that.'

Her expression changed. 'But when you threw at me what you did—oh, God, I didn't have the strength for that. How could I have? What you hurled at me—what I thought you were accusing me of—I could not defend myself against that. Because I knew…knew that what I'd wanted so much was to be taken into my father's family, not to be rejected by them any more. But you made me see it was impossible—that I was just a sordid little secret from Ian's father's past...'

Athan groaned and held her away from him, only the better to talk to her. His hands slipped to her shoulders.

'I would never have objected to you for that reason alone. Yes, Ian's mother suffered—but that was not your fault. How could it be? *Nothing* has been your fault. Only mine.' His voice was heavy. 'Only mine.'

She heard the self-accusation in his voice and hated it.

'No.' Her negation was fierce. 'I will not let you say that. I will not let you...or me...look backwards now. I let anger blind me—blind me into rejecting you.' She clutched him suddenly, clinging to him urgently. 'Oh, I so nearly let you walk away from me. Don't ever, *ever* let me be so blind again!'

'Every time you look at me,' he promised her, his voice warm and rich and full of all he felt for her, 'you'll see my love for you. It will be your mirror for all time. A true mirror. That I promise you.'

Her gaze was troubled suddenly. 'It *hurt*,' she said. 'It hurt so much to realise that all the time you knew me in London, all the time we had on holiday, it was just...fake. The whole thing. When I thought it was real...'

Now the negation was his—and fiercer.

'It *was*—it was real! That was the whole torment of it all! Knowing that if it weren't for Eva, for what I thought I was doing to save her marriage, I would be spending that time with you without that hanging over my head. That's why I so arrogantly thought I could get you back again—get that time back again. Oh, God, Marisa, to hold you in my arms again—to have you for myself this time, *only* myself. With no other reason to get in the way of us.' He gazed down at her, emotion pouring from him. 'And now...finally...after all this time...there truly is nothing to part us...to confuse and confound and blind us. Now—oh, my most beloved girl—there really is only this...'

He kissed her. Tenderly. Carefully. Lovingly.

'Only this,' he murmured.

He eased her away from him, changing his hold on her to put an arm around her shoulder, holding her hand in his across his body as he started to walk her along the path again. Side by side.

Peace filled her. Peace she had not felt for so long. A peace that she knew now would last for ever.

'What fools we've been,' she said dreamily, leaning her head against his shoulder.

He gave a low laugh. 'Me more than you.'

She shook her head. 'No, me more than you.'

He glanced down at her. 'You'll have to grant me the privilege of being right this time around.' He dropped a kiss on her hair.

'Uh-uh.'

He lanced the quirking smile at her that made her heart turn over—her tumbled, jangled heart that had finally found its resting place.

'An argumentative woman, are you?' he teased. 'Well, there is only one way to settle it. You shall be right, my darling, all the time henceforth. Will that keep you happy?'

She shook her head. 'Only one thing will keep me happy.'

'Oh?' he queried, his smile tugging deeper. 'And what will that be?'

'You,' she said. 'Only you. For all time.' Love blazed from her eyes. A fire that could never be quenched.

'Done,' he answered. 'And shall I seal the deal like this?'

Their kiss was long and deep and stronger than time.

Which stood still all around them and always would.

EPILOGUE

'READY?'

Athan's tone was a mix of encouragement and support. His arm, to which Marisa was clinging tightly, was steady as a rock. A rock she knew she could always lean on—all her life. Including this evening.

'OK, let's do it,' he said.

He started forward, opening the door and leading the way into the room beyond. Marisa was conscious of a slight increase in her heart rate, but that was only to be expected. She walked in, Athan at her side. Together they paused on the threshold.

'Marisa!' Ian's voice was warm and welcoming as he hurried up to them. He bestowed his golden smile on her, and kissed her lightly on the cheek.

His smile encompassed Athan as well, and Athan returned it. His regard for his brother-in-law had increased dramatically now that he was assured that nothing of Martin Randall's faithless nature was in him. Ian had proved increasingly loyal and steadfast, working hard to make his new job a success, and ensuring Eva was the happiest wife in the world.

Almost the happiest, he amended, and his glance down at Marisa at his side was rich and full with love. He felt his heart constrict. How very much he loved her! She was the centre of his world—the other half of his being...

'Marisa?'

Ian's voice interrupted Athan's reverie.

'This is a moment I have longed for. Will you take my hand?'

Still with an edge of tension inside her, Marisa placed her free hand in Ian's and he closed his fingers tightly over hers. The three of them walked forward to the figure standing by the ornate fireplace on the far side of the drawing room in Ian's family house. Though her vision was focussed on the figure standing there Marisa was conscious of Eva, sitting in the armchair beside the fire, smiling encouragingly at her.

For a moment as Marisa approached she thought she saw a tension in the features of the figure's face that equalled her own. She could understand its cause only too well. Then once more Ian was speaking. Not this time to Marisa, but to the older woman.

'This is Marisa,' he said. His voice was level, his gaze steady. 'My sister.'

For a moment time seemed to hang still. Then, with a little sound in her throat, Sheila Randall broke the tension. She held out her hands to Marisa.

'My dear,' she said. Her voice was rich with emotion.

As Marisa took the outstretched hands, dropping her hold on both Athan and her brother, she felt an answering emotion well up in her. In Sheila Randall's face was nothing but kindness—and the haunting of past sorrows.

Her hands pressed Marisa's. Her eyes looked deep into hers. 'I sincerely believe,' she said, 'that your poor mother suffered as greatly as I did, and for that reason I know I can never blame her or accuse her.' There was a choke in her voice now. 'I can only be glad that Ian found you. So glad that you are part of our family,' she said. Her gaze went to Athan. 'I can think of no happier ending,' she said.

Marisa's hands slipped from hers, took Athan's waiting hands instead, and felt their warmth and strength flow through her.

'Nor I,' she agreed.

And love, like a swelling tide, swept through her.

With eyes only for her, his beloved, Athan lifted Marisa's hands to his mouth, kissing them one after another, holding them close against his heart.

'Nor I,' he said.

For an endless, timeless moment their eyes poured into each other's. Then a soft pop drew their attention back to their surroundings.

'Time for champagne,' said Ian.

Eva was there in an instant, holding out glasses to be filled with the gently fizzing liquid. When all the glasses were charged, Ian lifted his first, to give the toast.

'To Athan and Marisa,' he said. 'And the triumph of true love.'

It was a toast that no one there objected to.

* * * * *

Mills & Boon® Hardback

October 2012

ROMANCE

Banished to the Harem	Carol Marinelli
Not Just the Greek's Wife	Lucy Monroe
A Delicious Deception	Elizabeth Power
Painted the Other Woman	Julia James
A Game of Vows	Maisey Yates
A Devil in Disguise	Caitlin Crews
Revelations of the Night Before	Lynn Raye Harris
Defying her Desert Duty	Annie West
The Wedding Must Go On	Robyn Grady
The Devil and the Deep	Amy Andrews
Taming the Brooding Cattleman	Marion Lennox
The Rancher's Unexpected Family	Myrna Mackenzie
Single Dad's Holiday Wedding	Patricia Thayer
Nanny for the Millionaire's Twins	Susan Meier
Truth-Or-Date.com	Nina Harrington
Wedding Date with Mr Wrong	Nicola Marsh
The Family Who Made Him Whole	Jennifer Taylor
The Doctor Meets Her Match	Annie Claydon

MEDICAL

A Socialite's Christmas Wish	Lucy Clark
Redeeming Dr Riccardi	Leah Martyn
The Doctor's Lost-and-Found Heart	Dianne Drake
The Man Who Wouldn't Marry	Tina Beckett

Mills & Boon® Large Print

October 2012

ROMANCE

A Secret Disgrace	Penny Jordan
The Dark Side of Desire	Julia James
The Forbidden Ferrara	Sarah Morgan
The Truth Behind his Touch	Cathy Williams
Plain Jane in the Spotlight	Lucy Gordon
Battle for the Soldier's Heart	Cara Colter
The Navy SEAL's Bride	Soraya Lane
My Greek Island Fling	Nina Harrington
Enemies at the Altar	Melanie Milburne
In the Italian's Sights	Helen Brooks
In Defiance of Duty	Caitlin Crews

HISTORICAL

The Duchess Hunt	Elizabeth Beacon
Marriage of Mercy	Carla Kelly
Unbuttoning Miss Hardwick	Deb Marlowe
Chained to the Barbarian	Carol Townend
My Fair Concubine	Jeannie Lin

MEDICAL

Georgie's Big Greek Wedding?	Emily Forbes
The Nurse's Not-So-Secret Scandal	Wendy S. Marcus
Dr Right All Along	Joanna Neil
Summer With A French Surgeon	Margaret Barker
Sydney Harbour Hospital: Tom's Redemption	Fiona Lowe
Doctor on Her Doorstep	Annie Claydon

0912 GEN STD LP

ROMANCE

A Night of No Return	Sarah Morgan
A Tempestuous Temptation	Cathy Williams
Back in the Headlines	Sharon Kendrick
A Taste of the Untamed	Susan Stephens
Exquisite Revenge	Abby Green
Beneath the Veil of Paradise	Kate Hewitt
Surrendering All But Her Heart	Melanie Milburne
Innocent of His Claim	Janette Kenny
The Price of Fame	Anne Oliver
One Night, So Pregnant!	Heidi Rice
The Count's Christmas Baby	Rebecca Winters
His Larkville Cinderella	Melissa McClone
The Nanny Who Saved Christmas	Michelle Douglas
Snowed in at the Ranch	Cara Colter
Hitched!	Jessica Hart
Once A Rebel...	Nikki Logan
A Doctor, A Fling & A Wedding Ring	Fiona McArthur
Her Christmas Eve Diamond	Scarlet Wilson

MEDICAL

Maybe This Christmas…?	Alison Roberts
Dr Chandler's Sleeping Beauty	Melanie Milburne
Newborn Baby For Christmas	Fiona Lowe
The War Hero's Locked-Away Heart	Louisa George

Mills & Boon® Large Print

November 2012

ROMANCE

HISTORICAL

MEDICAL